MAY YOUR GIFTS BE HIS

A TAKERS NOVELLA

LOGAN SROUFE

COSMIC FROG MEDIA, LTD

For information regarding subsidiary rights, please get in touch with the Publisher.

Cosmic Frog Media, LTD

8666 Beechmont Ave #1047

Cincinnati, OH 45255

www.logansroufe.com

Editing services by Fleetwood Robbins

Cover illustration by El Huervo

Cover design by Steph Hess

ISBN: 979-8-9920906-0-4

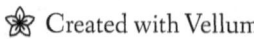 Created with Vellum

To Becky

CONTENTS

1 / ALPHA

ALPHA STOOD OVER HER BUNK, a frown reflecting from the helmet in her hands. A black visor flush against the surrounding armor plating, the helmet appeared as a singular piece of polished obsidian. Her body from the neck down was clad in kind, yet she moved as if wearing silk. The case she retrieved it from was empty, aside from a featureless black dagger—her misericorde. The suit appeared brand new, replacing her previous set that was damaged beyond repair during her last deployment. Nevertheless, she scrutinized it for familiar scratches that didn't exist.

"How does it feel?" Djonah asked, setting his helmet down.

"Strange, it feels like my old one," Alpha mumbled. She stretched out her right hand and flexed her forearm, the suit effortlessly in alignment with her musculature. Silky strands of blonde hair draped over her bicep as she opened and closed her fist, so she tossed her head back to move them out of the way. She smiled, briefly reminiscing about the deaths of several traitorous clones by her hand until she noticed she had an audience.

"Looks brand new," Djonah smirked, raising his arm to compare.

Alpha swatted it away and returned to admiring the crafts-manship and beauty of her new suit. "Don't ruin this for me," she sighed. "Though, awarding me this new suit is strange considering the ceremony today. I wonder if I'll get to keep it once I become the pilot."

Djonah shrugged and backed away, returning to his bunk a few feet across the room in silence. He began to collect his helmet and misericorde from a similar—yet worn—case, tossing his blade to the edge of the bunk.

"You didn't forget about the pilot ceremony, did you?"Alpha lowered her arm. The mortified young man wasn't making eye contact. "Look at me, Djonah."

Djonah snapped his head up and stared at her, his eyes wide. Alpha stepped closer to inspect her subordinate. She admired his attention to grooming detail and cropped hair, which was alluring in how different it was from hers. The outline of his spongy freeform locs reminded her of a gathering thunderhead, the kind of cloud that preceded a violent storm.

She wrapped an armored palm around the back of his skull and pulled him down to her height. As for flaws with his groom-ing, it was difficult to find any, but she noticed herself returning to his heterochromatic eyes. The dark suit, the dark skin, the dark hair. The one dark brown eye. The ice-blue iris amidst all the rest. It was a magnet for her attention, and Alpha returned to the eye again and again as she looked him up and down. She drew even closer, taking in his scent. Her eyes fluttered. She licked her lips close to Djonah's ear, letting warm air brush against it, lingering.

"Acceptable." She whispered, releasing him. "Now put on your helmet, Thaumaturge, before I order you to remove what you're already wearing. You're lucky this is a ceremony I don't want to miss."

Djonah complied and fumbled about until he found the opening of his helmet, then shunted it over his head. The humming of his misericorde overshadowed a faint hiss of suction as the helmet sealed itself around Djonah's neck. The obsidian dagger pulled itself from his bunk and affixed to the back of his waistline. Djonah relaxed, folded his arms behind his back, and stood with his legs comfortably apart. The shift in his confidence was immediate.

"Zeta!" Djonah called out into the cramped barracks room. His voice thudded through the digital voice amplifier within his helmet.

"May your gifts be his," Alpha responded, nodding as Djonah's visor began to shift in appearance. One at a time, seven bright chartreuse dots appeared in four rows on the glossy visor of his helmet—a row of two dots, then one, then two more, and finally, another two. The dots then shrank and rested within a small space upon his forehead, delineating Djonah's rank within his brotherhood. The visor obscured his face. Alpha's reflection, however, was visible as she leaned in close. They were face to face now, Alpha looking up at the taller Thaumaturge. She touched the lowest dots with a finger and then slipped it down his visor and neck, tracing almost imperceivable lines on his dark armor until she paused at a blemish on his right shoulder.

She cocked her head to the side, "What happened here?" Alpha pressed the blemish and noted how deep the wound must have been to leave such a mark. "This is new. You bled from this."

Djonah didn't respond, and his body went rigid. Traces of silver shimmered from within the scar. Alpha smiled and kept tracing her finger away from the wound along his chest and down his stomach, pausing again above his waistline.

"You were wounded too in our last deployment? Poor baby. I haven't had time to review the combat logs. I've been too excited about the upcoming ceremony. And here I thought you'd abandoned me during our last mission. I always knew you were a good boy." The rest of her hand joined Alpha's finger as she moved it further down beneath Djonah's waist and cupped her palm around his codpiece.

Djonah stepped back. "I..."

Alpha's hand jumped to where Djonah's mouth would be, and she pressed a finger there to silence him. He was always prone to self-deprecation; it was beneath such a warrior.

"Djonah, you may be the youngest of us, but you are far from the least worthy of my affections," Alpha cooed as she turned back to her bunk, taking the blade from the open case and affixing it to the back of her waistline. "You're the only one of us who has been training since birth, something I am equally jealous of and disgusted by. You have many skills I wish I had at your age. I imagine you will go on to do great things for Paran. If..." She paused, her eyes lingering on the wounded shoulder.

Djonah regained his composure. "If what?"

"If you survive."

Alpha retrieved a thick silver ring from underneath her pillow. She held it in her hand until a small amount of clear, viscous liquid pooled. She retrieved the ring and held it out for Djonah. "Hold this."

Djonah took the ring as instructed but left his arm outstretched as if offering it back to Alpha.

Alpha then rubbed her hands together and combed her wet, armored fingers through her lengthy hair, ensuring that the finer threads near her ears and at the nape of her neck got most of the solution. Her hair draped beneath her shoulders as she gathered it to form a ponytail. She twisted and then wrapped the flowing hair into a tight bun, tucking the tips underneath a familiar tuft on top of her head. Her throat was exposed as she worked with her hands, yet she never took her eyes off Djonah. She delighted in toying with him like this, pretending to be vulnerable. She loved how well-behaved he was—such a good boy. Smiling to herself, Alpha used one hand to clamp down on the bun and outstretched the other, palm open.

"Give it here," Alpha said as she took the ring back from Djonah, resting it on top of the bun she held with her other hand. She released them both as the ring ejected a restraining mesh that cinched around the entire bun before it could undo itself. Alpha felt around her head to ensure everything was in place, then grabbed her helmet.

She looked at Djonah, wondering if this would be the last time he'd get to watch her get dressed. Perhaps this evening's festivities may not go as planned. Alpha found herself growing fond of the young soldier despite his inadequacies. She envied his upbringing; the boy was barely a man, yet Djonah had seen and fought in more combat than most twice his age. She smirked, again forgetting that he was right there in the room, staring back at her.

"Are you alright?" Djonah asked, standing tall.

Alpha ignored him, slipping on her helmet and waiting for it to fasten around her neck before she spoke. "The ceremony is about to begin, Djonah. I don't know who will be selected to replace me, but I'm sure you will be left in capable hands."

"I hope so," Djonah said, relaxing his stance a bit. His voice sounded clear again, as their helmets were now connected via a secure comm link.

"I'm going to miss times like these," Alpha said, her helmet's single dot appearing in the center of her vision before rising beyond where she could see. The room began to wash out in a dark haze that lifted once the helmet's sensors and vision enhancements were initialized. Alpha took a deep breath as her suit's filtration system piped fresh oxygen into the small space between her face and the visor.

Bright colors began to cascade over the world in a blur. With each color came more layers of depth until everything appeared almost hyperreal, with objects appearing much more vibrant than they were seconds before. Djonah's suit now had purple shadows and deep lines of indigo that accentuated the curves of his form-fitting body armor. Her visor also highlighted the superficial damage his suit must have sustained in their previous deployment, represented by spiderwebs of microfissures on his chest. There was another spot on his left thigh, near his groin. She licked her lips.

"How are those healing?" Alpha asked, pointing to the larger fissures on Djonah's chest.

"I'm fine, Val. I'm sure they'll be completely healed before my next deployment," Djonah said, bowing his head and touching the mark before returning to his previous confident stance. "I mean, Alpha."

Alpha smirked. "Don't worry about it, Djonah. When it's just us, you can call me by my name. But not during the ceremony. I don't want you making any trouble for me." She was going to become a pilot today. A Holy Pilot, no less.

A crimson light began glowing from a glass dome nestled halfway into the ceiling, signaling the imminent ceremony. "It's time, Djonah."

Alpha walked toward the room's only visible door, which slid open as she approached, disappearing into the wall. She stopped before she left, turning to her inferior, who was a step or two behind. She pushed him aside, hoping to see her stats one last time. There were two small bunks along opposite walls, then one mirror display wall, and the wall she stood closest to was the unit statistics wall. It displayed all sorts of analytic feedback regarding previous deployments. She checked if her kill count was visible, but it was blank. The wall displayed a single sentence in bold red lettering above the door:

MAY YOUR GIFTS BE HIS.

Alpha tapped on Djonah's shoulder and pointed at the message. "Don't ever forget that."

Djonah glanced at the message and stepped closer, bending

as if to whisper in her ear. "I don't think I could if I wanted to," he mused, half laughing as he reached for Alpha's shoulder.

Alpha lurched back at the comment before shoving Djonah back into the room, the door sliding shut behind them. "Do not speak that way about Paran," she hissed. Djonah backed away, raising his arms in the sign of peace. "If the wrong person heard that kind of language..." Alpha shook her head. "With your record, you likely don't have long before a promotion yourself, so don't throw it all away by being careless with your mouth." Djonah was still a child in many ways—a shame.

"I'll behave," Djonah said, his arms still raised. "It was a bad joke, that's all. I'm sorry, Val."

Alpha sighed and made her way back to the door. "We aren't on the battlefield. You can't speak that way within the city limits. Just keep your mouth shut until the ceremony ends," Alpha growled as she strode away.

The long corridor before her was empty, aside from mirrored walls and ambient ceiling panels to light the way. She marched forward as Djonah kept close behind, but further than usual. She admired herself as she walked, smiling at the warrior in the mirror. Fond memories of glorious combat against ridiculous odds filled her mind. The shame of being crushed in her last deployment was buried beneath the mountain of otherwise endless victories.

As she approached, the door at the end of the hall opened, and another subordinate stood inside the dimly lit room beyond. She stepped through and nodded to the soldier, who nodded back. The Thaumaturge wore the same armor as she and

Djonah, but their helmet had two dots, one on top of the other. Beta.

The dome's curved walls were blanketed in dusty mounds of melted wax, with a lit pillar candle atop each of the seven mounds. Parchment scrolls whose writings had faded beyond recognition dangled from the dark ceiling. A well-trodden walkway surrounded seven supple padded chairs, all bolted to the floor in a horseshoe pattern and facing inward. In the center was a dim Holovid projector ring. Soft microsuede fabric lined every surface of Alpha's chair, and she took her seat at the center of the curve before nodding to Djonah and Beta to sit. They did.

Moments later, two other doors opened, and four identical Thaumaturges made their way in and sat down in the remaining empty chairs. The minimal lighting in the room dimmed once the final Thaumaturge took their seat, and the center of the room began to shift as the Holovid projector began to reveal an image. It was of a pale, elderly man leaning on a cane and smiling at nobody in particular. He wore a burgundy tunic and a pair of bronze-colored slacks underneath. Intricate patterns were woven along both garments, dancing on the silken fabric as the hologram turned. The man gazed upon each warrior.

"My great warriors," Paran said. "Thank you for your gifts. Your bravery is the blood that flows through the beating heart of my city. You have all kept your promise to me, and I honor you now for doing so."

The silent warriors said nothing in response, and the hologram smiled before turning to Alpha. "This is a momentous day. I've gathered you here for a special ceremony."

Alpha smiled, nodding to the hologram.

"It is time to reveal that we have now completed the final tests on my greatest achievement, TAKER 7," Paran said as he turned away from Alpha.

The hologram faded, and an image of a humanoid yet featureless body appeared in the center of the room. Paran's voice returned: "This is TAKER 7, and you are the first Thaumaturges to witness this titan in its final form. TAKER 7 is being held off-world for final checks but will be coming here shortly to welcome one of you as its Holy Pilot."

Alpha shifted in her chair, unable to resist the excitement. This was her ceremony. To become a Holy Pilot of a TAKER. She had always dreamed of being selected. Each TAKER took years, sometimes decades, to be completed. During her tenure as Alpha of the Black Thaumaturges, she had heard whispers of previous fellow Alphas being chosen to become pilots, but now it was about to become a reality. Her daydream was interrupted by Paran's voice.

"Hear me now, my great warriors. Hear the voice of Paran as I tell you why this moment is special to me," he said as the hologram of TAKER 7 rotated in front of the seven darkened soldiers. "TAKER 7 is the last of its kind. Alas, we no longer command enough precious resources to continue building such titans. Yet, with great joy, I announce to you, my great warriors, that TAKER 7 will be sent to a place rife with the materials and minerals we need to continue to build these colossi. That place is the great planet Cora."

A few Thaumaturges in the room shifted in their chairs; even Alpha gasped behind her visor at the announcement. Cora has always been beyond Paran's reach, and the planet is massive —it's the largest known planet in existence, no doubt swarming with enemy infestation and who knows what else. Yet the whelp remains calm.

"I know this may shock some of you, but as I said, we have no choice. Cora is not only our hope of replenishing desperately needed resources, but it may also be a world on which my great city could be reborn," Paran said as the hologram switched back to himself, and he was still smiling. "Only one of you will be selected as Holy Pilot, but the rest will still play a vital role. The Black Thaumaturges will become the Holy Pilot's keepers, their Constellation, a hidden support team that will orbit Cora in stasis until called upon. That is why it has to be all of you, my great warriors, as we need our deadliest soldiers to guarantee success in such a perilous endeavor."

This announcement caused more shifting in seats, but Alpha snapped forward and stared down at those who squirmed until they all, one by one, sat still. The hologram paused until Alpha sank back into her chair.

"I am not heartless." Paran clapped his hands together. "I know this is not what you expected to hear, yet I still believe it is a cause for celebration. Please take a moment to discuss this wonderful news with yourselves, and then we will continue. Any surviving next of kin have already been notified and will be greatly rewarded for your sacrifice. Your gifts that lift Paran's greatness into the future will never be forgotten. As we speak, a mural of the Black Thaumaturges is being commissioned to adorn the seventh wing of my largest cathedral. Congratulations."

The hologram disappeared, and the dim lights returned. A few of the soldiers looked back and forth before Beta stood up. "We knew this was a possibility, albeit a rare one. Our promise will bring great honor to us all and our brotherhood. May your gifts be his."

A soldier with five dots, Epsilon, hesitated before snapping their head toward Alpha, their right leg bouncing. "None of us will break our promise. After everything we've been through, I cannot believe that we are to be nothing more than frozen satellites, left to drift in orbit around a world so distant that not even Paran has been able to capture it. No TAKER has ever gone that deep into space. My family will be long dead before we can even hope to capture such a wild planet. Besides, when does a TAKER need any ground support? They crush entire civilizations in mere days. It pains me to feel so insignificant. We have so much more to give."

"I hear you, brother," Digamma, with six dots on their helmet, stood up. "This is truly a shock, but our names will be carved into history forever. We always knew there would be a time when we would likely have to lay down our lives to keep our promise. Is this so different? Think of the glory, and imagine the outcome if we succeed. Our planet is dying, and Cora is the only hope for our survival. I've even heard whispers that you can breathe without a helmet on its surface!"

Alpha waited for anyone else to speak. The soldiers stared back at her in silence, except for Djonah, whose calm indifference was becoming rather annoying.

"Something on your mind, Zeta?" Alpha said as Djonah stared between his feet, unresponsive. She stood up and raised her voice. "Look at me, Djonah." She knew he hated it when she used his name in front of the others.

"May your gifts be his," Djonah blurted out, lifting his head toward her.

"May your gifts be his," Alpha replied, nodding as the standing soldiers returned to their seats, waiting for the ceremony to continue in complete silence. Alpha was the last to sit.

"Let us continue," Paran's voice warbled from hidden speakers within the dome's walls. The floor flickered, and the hologram of TAKER 7 reappeared, zooming in close to the titan's face. It had three large, circular, yellow eyes in two rows on either side of its head, with a much larger and ornate eye resting upon its forehead. The hologram began to zoom out, and long cords of multicolored materials draped down from its skull in what appeared to be a ponytail. The vibrant hair and eyes stood out on an otherwise dull and unremarkable body. The few discernible characteristics below the neck were the human-like hands and a feminine curvature around the chest and hips. Alpha beamed beneath her visor, glancing down at her own body. TAKER 7 must have been modeled after her future pilot.

"TAKER 7, while being the last of its kind, is also the first of its kind in many ways. Its promise is to ensure the gift of Cora for me. The rest of you chosen to become its Constellation will ensure the Holy Pilot's success. The Holy Pilot will channel their warrior spirit into the very limbs of this magnificent creation and show whatever resistance awaits you on Cora that Paran's Empire has arrived. That Cora's gifts are needed. This

Holy Pilot's will alone will bring any resistance to heel, which is why I've come to you, my great warriors. Who better than you who are relentlessly seeking out and destroying the traitors here within my planet?" Paran wheezed, then composed himself. "Now, where were we?"

Small red pillars of light spotlighted each of the seven soldiers.

"The Holy Pilot of TAKER 7 has been selected," Paran announced, digital music creeping into a crescendo behind his words as Alpha's stomach churned. She couldn't believe there was wetness in her eyes, something so foreign she'd almost forgotten the sensation. The intensity of the music rose along with the red lighting, and Paran's hologram used this moment to walk around the circle of Thaumaturges. He paused before each of them and returned to the center of the ring. Paran smiled as the musical number concluded, closing his eyes to enjoy the coda before the synthetic symphony faded into silence. Alpha was almost shivering as Paran walked toward her.

She held her breath.

"Alpha, you have always been the bravest and fiercest amongst these great warriors, and until your last deployment, you had never known defeat," Paran said. "I'm sure the rest of your brothers would agree that you are the deadliest in the room, myself included," Paran laughed.

Alpha nodded to the hologram, but something sharp and icy coiled in her stomach. She compared her spotless armor to the imperfect blemishes on those around her. She snapped in a tiny breath and then held it again. It didn't mean anything. Her armor was crushed beyond repair after that fall into the elevator shaft, and nobody could have guessed that one of those clones would have had advanced combat training and such high-security clearance. She had nearly lost her life being buried beneath the massive elevator that was dropped on her from hundreds of stories above. If only Djonah had been there like he was supposed to be, none of that would have happened.

"Nevertheless," Paran said as the icy coil gave way to total panic, her teeth clenching. "TAKER 7, as I said, is the first of its kind. It, of course, requires a pilot who is the first of its kind."

The hologram disappeared and then reappeared in front of Djonah. "Zeta, you have been chosen to become the Holy Pilot of TAKER 7. The rest of you are to become his Constellation. Zeta, you were chosen for this long before birth, hence your prestigious upbringing amongst your fellow warriors. All of that suffering was to prepare you for this very moment. Congratulations, Djonah, and congratulations to you all. Alpha will still lead the Constellation, but Djonah is no longer beholden to any of your authority, only mine."

The hologram paused, and the room was washed in a profound silence. Djonah stared at the older man, but Alpha refused to breathe, frozen. Her suit reacted by deploying chemicals into her bloodstream to counteract the high levels of cortisol it had detected, and she soon found herself back in hazy control of her faculties. She took a deep breath and shuddered. Her jaw ached.

"May your gifts be his..." Alpha choked out as she stared toward Djonah along with every other Thaumaturge in the room. The red pillars of light disappeared, aside from the one still shining over the Holy Pilot of TAKER 7. Djonah lowered his gaze to the floor and remained silent.

The final pillar disappeared, darkening the room aside from Paran's hologram and the flickering candles beyond the warriors.

"Details will be delivered to your rooms shortly. Djonah, you will stay behind as you are to begin the rituals of the Holy Pilot immediately. An envoy is already en route to collect you so that you may begin. That is all."

The lights in the room snapped on as the hologram disappeared, and Alpha found herself standing up and meandering back toward the hallway from which she had come, the drugs calming her mind. "May your gifts be his. Dismissed," she mumbled. The rest of the Thaumaturges rose and shuffled back toward their rooms. Alpha paused inside the mirrored hall and spun back to Djonah, the Holy Pilot still sitting in his chair. Sitting where she was meant to be. "You knew, didn't you?"

"I don't want to be a pilot. I'm sorry I didn't tell you." Djonah stared at the floor. "I couldn't. You—"

The door between them closed abruptly, and the secure comm link between their helmets was severed.

Alpha screamed and fell to the ground, pounding her fists against the floor, the taste of copper in her mouth.

2 / REZ

REZ TIP-TOED up the crumbling steps of a long abandoned cathedral, unable to let go of the scowl on his face. The desolation was all-encompassing. Billowing clouds of dust blew across the stairs, forcing him to shield his face until the wind subsided. He looked beyond the cathedral toward the silent buildings in the distance, unsure if they were empty. They looked empty. Unease crept in. The entire sector around the gated cathedral was vacant—long abandoned since the last time he'd set foot here. How had he not known? He should have picked another meeting place, somewhere less desolate. The fond memories of lush hanging gardens and delectable aromas of the open market were marred by this new reality.

Paran had called Rez home for the first time in over a hundred years, tasked to test the mettle of the new Holy Pilot that would be locked inside TAKER 7. Djonah was to be tested in combat. Who knew what waited for him on Cora? Paran needed to know if his new pilot was up to the task and if not, well...

Rez finished his climb and came upon two massive bronze doors, their ornate carvings covered in a mottled red, green, and copper patina. One of the doors was ajar, so he slipped through. Inside the main chamber, he looked up, gazing at the magnificent ceiling ornamentation, which was still wholly transparent, albeit dirty. The night sky was cloudless, and the moon shone down upon his face.

Bright lights shifted about in the sky, into and away from even larger, stationary lights. Those were the Orbit Crawlers. Boyish memories of watching Paran's Orbit Crawlers parading in an orderly line, moving to and from outer space, made Rez smile. He would watch one for as long as possible until it disappeared above the clouds. It was strange not seeing any of the dots coming back down from the heavens like they used to. Rez looked down at the rest of the cathedral and frowned.

There were small piles of rubble about the massive granite walls, and most of the wooden seating had rotted and collapsed. The crimson floors were now a faded pastel pink. He took a few more steps in and noticed the Black Thaumaturge he was to meet leaning against a cracked marble pillar not far away. They wore a sleek armored suit and matching helmet, with seven green dots adorned at the top of their visor. The Thaumaturge quickly snapped to a more confident stance once Rez made himself known. That must be Djonah. Born long after the world's better days—what a miserable life he must have had, raised by warriors, haunted by stories of a world far more bountiful than the one he was brought into.

"Give me a moment," Rez said before taking a deep breath and staring at the altar towards the end of the room. A broken yet still ornate throne sat upon it, the colorful artistry having long since turned into muted tones of flat beige. The grand achievements of Paran and his heroes no longer adorned the massive panels of the throne, causing wistful feelings to swell inside Rez's mind. This had been the most inspiring place once. And now? Look at what had happened to it while he'd been away. What a shame it is to see it in this pitiful state.

Rez walked up to the throne and gently caressed the broken stone with an outstretched silver hand. His matching silken armor hadn't changed nearly as much as the ground where he stood. Rez's suit and many long spans of hypersleep had kept him alive unnaturally long. He mused that it gave him this strange opportunity to return to places of his youth, hundreds of years later, and stand in the empty rubble of what once was.

A crunch of rubble startled Rez. Djonah was walking down the cathedral aisle, approaching the throne.

"My apologies, Djonah. I'd introduce myself, but I'm sure you already know who I am." Rez laughed, taking a few steps down from the altar toward the Black Thaumaturge. "This place holds so many memories for me. To see it like this is more difficult than I'd like to admit. I hoped to inspire you with its grandeur, and I had not realized it lay in ruin."

Djonah paused. "We can go somewhere else. I thought I was being deployed along with the rest of my team to Paran's Citadel to handle a clone uprising, but then I found out about this meeting, and my transport rerouted me here."

"Oh, don't worry," Rez interrupted. "This is fine. I

wanted a place where we could be alone, and well..." Rez trailed off, opening his arms to the room. He paused to muse at the altar throne and pointed toward it. "Confessor Yuza used to sit there and tell incredible stories of how Paran came to be. She told us about the two TAKERS, one of which still strides the border of this great city. Ever since I learned about them, I wanted to become a pilot. But it all started here, for me."

Rez didn't notice, but he'd begun to frown. "Hundreds of years later, and everyone I know has gone. Aside from Paran and the other pilots and crew, of course. Piloting TAKER 3 has been a great honor. I hope to one day see this place restored once we have given Paran enough gifts. That is why your mission is so important."

Djonah stood next to Rez and craned his neck toward a faded mural. Rez put a hand on Djonah's shoulder and smiled. "These murals were my favorite part. So many fables were told within them, layering stories upon one other. I wish you could have seen it. Whatever digital replicas you may have encountered on a console could never match seeing it with your own eyes." Rez looked at Djonah, suddenly uncomfortable seeing his reflection in the side of the Thaumaturge's black helmet. Curly blonde hair fell upon his bony, pale face, and Rez gasped at himself. So old. So much time has gone. The pale blue eyes in the reflection were dull.

Djonah turned, giving up on the mural and startling Rez. "How long has it been since you've stepped foot in this cathedral?"

Rez closed his eyes, then cocked his head to the side, the

corner of his mouth suddenly twitching. The innocuous question clawed deep into his mind, causing him to shudder.

"I didn't—" Djonah raised a hand, but Rez waved his own as if to brush away any concern.

"I'm not sure exactly, maybe... two hundred years?" Rez said as gracefully as he could, gritting his teeth. "No apologies necessary; you may experience similar feelings in due time. It is a strange burden all pilots must endure. We experience the passage of time in ways few can fathom. I feel as if my future is behind me."

Although maybe it wouldn't be that way for Djonah. TAKER 7 was going further than anyone ever had, equipped with specialized technology that no one was permitted to know the details of—just that it would be an aid. And Djonah even had a Holy Fixer assigned to him, which would be company, at least. Perhaps he'd be spared this strange, prolonged loneliness.

Rez clapped his hands together, trying to distract himself and redirect the conversation. "Djonah. How has your training been progressing? I've read reports indicating that you are quite deadly at grappling. Dueling, however, you scored rather poorly. I'm assuming that is why I'm here. Did you know I was Paran's most decorated duelist before I became a pilot?"

"I'm not used to fighting that way." Djonah shrugged as he touched the weapon at the small of his back, adjusting it slightly. "There is no honor left in combat. I use stealth and camouflage mostly. Dueling is pointless when all of my targets have no chance of survival. They run and hide until they can't any longer."

Rez nodded, ignoring Djonah's tone. "That is your misericorde, yes?" Rez waved a delicate hand toward the hidden weapon. "Show me, will you? I've not seen one up close. They were developed long after I'd left this world inside TAKER 3, likely alongside the inconspicuous armor you wear."

Djonah nodded, removed the dagger from his waist, and presented it to Rez, who shook his head with slight disapproval.

"Show me *how it works*," Rez said, raising an eyebrow. He studied the peculiar weapon. "I want to see it transform."

"The dagger form is its default weapon." Djonah gripped the handle with his right hand. He squeezed the grip, and the dagger extended the hilt and blade to become a short sword. The thaumaturge held the weapon up and turned it to show off the double edge. "Still perfectly balanced, but now with better crowd control."

Rez nodded, admiring the uniformity. "There is one more weapon it may shift into, correct?" Politely asking even though he already knew the answer.

Djonah stepped back a few paces before the blade shot up as the handle shot down. The sword became a spear. "The spear I use mainly for def—" Djonah shook his head, sighing. "I throw it at runners."

"Incredible, an impressive gift!" Rez stepped toward Djonah, trying to move the awkward encounter along. "Now, I'm going to show you my gift." Rez raised his right hand as if offering something to Djonah. "Behold."

Rez straightened his silver hand and pressed his fingers together. Sterling liquid began to pool in the shallow cavity of his open hand. The fluid started to move on its own, spreading slowly as it flowed around his thumb and crept up along his fingertips. The liquid shot out and hardened immediately, changing his hand into a silver blade. The tip pointed toward Djonah.

"This was *my* gift from Paran." Rez twisted his blade hand before Djonah, showcasing how it shined even in the diffuse moonlight. "This rare material is the same that covers the hands of TAKER 3."

"Why don't any of the other TAKERS have those weapons?" Djonah asked, approaching Rez. "It seems after you, the others have all gone weaponless, with TAKER 1 being the only other to carry a sword of any kind.

Rez sighed, lowering the blade arm. "I'm told we lost the ability to refine the material needed to make it, and even after taking the planet responsible for the minerals and technology, unfortunately, the society decided to resist, so their cities were burned. With their society's death, so did the ability for Paran to manufacture and refine this wondrous material. TAKER 3 contains most of the material we found. I'm confident that one day, we will refine it again. The process, however, has proven to be more challenging than initially expected."

Djonah nodded. "My misericorde seems similar in a way," he said, holding up his weapon with both hands. He inspected the shaft and spear tip before tapping the blunt end into the floor.

"Yes, and I'm sure it is of high quality. This liquid, however, flows within me. It mixes within my blood and grants me such strange power. Centuries later, I'm still learning to blend with it both in and out of combat." He raised his other hand and created a matching blade. "I'm told the civilization that refined this material could form this liquid into any tool required, yet I only know how to create these. I often wish I could speak to one of them to learn how to make my hand into something other than a weapon."

Djonah nodded, admiring the display, but his gaze shifted to Rez's face. Rez smiled. His face flushed with the liquid, matching the color of his hands now. People were more often startled by his face than by the weapons he brandished.

"Spar with me, won't you, brother?" Rez said with the taste of metal on his tongue. "I've read about your exploits in the field of combat. Could you show me what fighting is like now? I'd love to show you what honorable combat can look like from someone who won't run. Pretend I'm one of those clones the rest of your brotherhood is off dealing with."

Rez lunged towards Djonah, not waiting for a response. The Thaumaturge stumbled back but slapped at Rez with the spear, clattering against his bladed hands. Djonah's face was utterly invisible behind his dark visor, but Rez thought he could see a pale blue eye staring wide back at him.

"First blood wins," Rez said, almost laughing. He leaped into the air, his muscles brimming with energy from the alien serum flowing through his veins. He grinned at the drastic spike in energy, his long-practiced martial arts showcasing a skill his dead masters could have only dreamed of.

Djonah's black suit vanished within the shadows, the Thaumaturge retreating into a dark corner away from Rez. "Stealth is an interesting choice," Rez cackled. He rushed into the dark, following Djonah. "Especially considering what you will be soon piloting. Do you think your TAKER can rely on such cowardly tricks?"

A black blade sliced from the darkness, barely missing Rez. The silver pilot bent forward and unnaturally pushed off the ground, turning his dodge into an attack. Rez thundered into Djonah's chest with his shoulder, sending the stunned Thaumaturge clattering back beneath the moonlight.

"TAKERS do not fight in the shadows. Neither should we," Rez said, ambling back into the open aisle where Djonah was coughing. "Now, get up and fight me in the open."

Djonah picked himself up with the sword, then lunged at Rez with a heavy thrust. Rez parried it with one hand, then sliced at Djonah with the other. The Thaumaturge released his weapon and fell away unscathed from the incoming strike. Djonah tumbled backward, quickly lifting an open hand towards Rez, and the ebony sword pulled itself back into his hand, ready to fight again.

"Well done!" Rez said, taking a deep breath, the cold and invigorating air filling his lungs. He began twisting and turning his body while dancing to a song he'd started humming. The cathedral's emptiness echoed the tune and the crunching sounds of rubble he trod upon. He playfully spun towards his confused opponent.

"What are you doing?" Djonah said, looking about. The humming reverberated around him.

"I'm dancing with you, Djonah," Rez slowed his movements along with the song. "You need music to dance. Dueling is very much a dance, you know. I've always dueled to this song." Rez sang out for a moment before returning to the hum.

"Music?" Djonah said before Rez advanced again.

"Yes," Rez chirped, jabbing at Djonah's shoulder, the pilot remaining still. The young Thaumaturge's armor took most of the attack, and Rez's arm buckled. He hadn't put much into the lunge, but Djonah's ability to sustain such a blow made Rez's arm rattle so hard that it broke his concentration on the tune he was humming.

Djonah didn't react aside from turning to his shoulder, which now had a small trickle of blood coming from it. He lifted his head back to Rez. "Can you keep doing that sound?" Almost immediately, the bleeding stopped, and the wound vanished behind a silvery blemish. The armor nearly appeared as if it hadn't been struck.

Rez squinted. "The song? Ah, no, I cannot. I apologize, brother! I was so lost in the moment that I forgot that music is now forbidden." He raised both bladed arms in the air, shrugging. "A strange rule, yet we live in strange times, do we not? Paran guides us through this nightmare, and we would do well to follow. I apologize."

Music being forbidden was an odd decision, a law enacted in the last fifty years or so long after Rez had been a Holy Pilot.

Djonah nodded, turning his sword back into a dagger. The darkened visor of his helmet began to shift into a more translucent gray, revealing his face. "I first heard something like it when Paran told me in secret a few days ago that I'd been selected as the new pilot. I'd never heard anything like it before. Music is its name, then. Paran told me there would be an official ceremony soon, witnessed by the rest of my brotherhood. He said I'd hear more music then, and once I'm a Holy Pilot, almost nothing would be forbidden to me. "

Rez sighed and began twisting his hands. The blades started to melt away into liquid, dripping backward into the palms of his hands. The power surge began to wane, and profound exhaustion took its place.

"Can you help me stand, brother?" Rez asked, raising his palms toward Djonah, who placed his misericorde back onto his waist. The Thaumaturge took Rez by hand and then braced the slumping silver duelist.

"I won, by the way," Rez said, letting himself sink into Djonah's support. "This gift is also a bit of a burden, it would seem, but after some rest, I'll be ready to go again. I'd love to try and spar with you again, and I promise not to sing next time. That was unfair."

"I wouldn't mind if you did," Djonah said, laughing softly as the two staggered toward the open cathedral door. "I liked how it sounded."

The two approached the exit, but Rez nudged against the new pilot. "Wait a moment."

Rez motioned to turn back to the throne, and Djonah helped him. Rez took a deep breath, memories flooding in as strength flooded away. Ghosts of a chanting congregation that once echoed throughout the now-barren cathedral brought a longing smile to his face. The memory sustained him even in the stark contrast of the ruins before him. Rez imagined the calming voice of Confessor Yuza calling out from the throne, and his eyes became wet.

"Are you alright?" Djonah asked, shifting his feet to take more weight off Rez.

"I'm alright, brother," Rez said softly, eyelids half open. "Seeing this place again, so many memories are returning to me. It is like..." Rez began to slump, then startled himself awake again. "Like a dream come true."

Rez lifted his head toward Djonah, who was all but carrying him at this point. "This is what we fight for, you know. This dream." Rez raised a limp finger to gesture at the cathedral, but it quickly fell.

Djonah took in the same view. A piece of rubble tumbled from the brittle ceiling, clattering near the throne before stopping on the drab and discolored red carpet. Djonah frowned and turned to look back at Rez, who had fallen asleep.

"May your gifts be his," Djonah whispered, lifting the silver pilot and carrying him down the crumbling steps of the cathedral towards the awaiting autonomous transport vehicle below.

3 / REMBLY

REMBLY'S TREMBLING hands clenched around the rigid armrests of his aluminum office chair. Three nested rings glowed above the center of his dilapidated aluminum desk. A holographic image of a green-robed figure appeared, blurry until the colors and finer details filtered in. It was Rembly's handler, Confessor Darsus.

"Confessor Rembly. I don't have time to speak, as a grave blasphemy was uncovered in the Citadel. The Black Thaumaturges have just arrived and..." Darsus trailed off. "The timeline is moving quicker than anticipated. I'm assuming you've read TAKER 7's Directives I sent earlier? Have you called for her yet?"

Rembly nodded but remained silent. Over and over again, he'd read them.

"Good. Lekki's transport is en route. Once she is collected, I will send further details regarding your reassignment. That is all. May your gifts be his."

The colorful rings dimmed, and the hologram dissipated. Rembly peeled his hands away from the chair and cupped them over his ears, the touch of his icy fingertips piercing through some of the shock. Pressing his heavy palms against his head to block out the incessant thrumming of the mining machinery beyond the walls of his office, Rembly instead tried to focus on the pulsating rhythm of his racing heart.

"No, no, not yet. Please..." Rembly whined into the dark room. It responded by automatically flicking on the overhead light as the rings on the table merged into the desk surface. The lights rose to their full brightness, forcing Rembly to squint. There was a faint knock at the door. She was here.

Rembly didn't respond. He couldn't.

He set his elbows on the now-empty table. "Table," he whispered, looking down at his dirty forest-green robes. "Robes," he said somewhat louder. They were older than he was, passed down to him from the last confessor that operated within this remote copper mine. Rembly was the second confessor stationed here and would be the last. The new directives all but confirmed it.

In truth, confessors were no longer necessary for Paran's influence. Yet their flourishing numbers had meant the handful of ceremonial positions remaining within the city were held by the most decorated or connected. The rest, like him, were sent off to barely habitable areas that contained a high likelihood of violent resistance or cult activity.

He'd even heard whispers of stubborn confessors being sent into space to proselytize distant worlds, no doubt captured or killed the moment they arrived in whatever civilization awaited them. Paran had quite the reputation at this point. Hands still pressed against his ears, he couldn't drown out the cacophony beyond the walls. "Noise!" Rembly growled, feeling a bit more confident.

There was another knock at the door.

Rembly pushed away from the table until his chair bumped into the wall. He frowned and attempted to stand, his belly pressing hard against the table edge. The cramped office was big enough for him, the table, and one guest. His visitors had the pleasure of sitting on a three-legged metal stool that liked to tip over. The room was otherwise barren aside from a harsh globe light suspended from the high ceiling and the phrase "May your gifts be his..." written in an ornate script of gold foil on the wall where Rembly's eyes naturally rested when sitting at his desk.

The guest knocked again, but softer this time.

"I'm coming," Rembly grumbled, shuffling toward the door. It wasn't far, but his long days in the confined space had left his back and joints so stiff that even these short distances had become a chore. He pressed his umber palm against the control panel, and the door slid open.

The silhouette of a young woman swallowed up the shadows of the mine beyond the doorway. Long black hair flowed around her obscure pale face. Wrinkled green overalls and oversized mining boots covered her lithe frame, and she carried a metallic jar in her gloved hands. She looked anywhere but at Rembly.

The confessor stared down at the young woman, who was less than half his age. Despite everything, he couldn't help but smile. It faded when she continued to keep her eyes away from him.

"Lekki, look at me," he blurted out, backing up. "Please come inside. It's warm in here."

Lekki didn't move. Instead, she shook her head and gripped the container tight to her chest. "Confessor, your hood is missing."

Rembly's eyes bulged at the realization. He grabbed the elastic fabric from around his neck, lifting it up and over his shaved head. He adjusted the mask until it lined up on his face so that around his eyes and mouth were dark patches of open weaving. This allowed him to see and speak without filtering too much of his vision or voice.

The thick canvas hood behind his head lifted over the mask to complete the uniform. Rembly cleared his throat. "There. Thank you for the reminder. Now, please, look upon me so that I might see your eyes one last time."

Lekki snapped her gaze to Rembly's covered face; her brown eyes were so deep that Rembly feared he might drown in them. Tears began to pool while he lingered, knowing everything was about to change.

"What are you talking about?" Lekki asked, stepping into the cramped room and placing the container on the table. With an expectant face, she stared at Rembly, who shut the door and shuffled toward his chair. The confessor took labored breaths through his mask and rested once he settled back into his seat.

"I will, but first, tell me what you've discovered today. Is it anything I might enjoy?" Rembly lifted the container, and, with a press of a button, the lid began to unscrew and open, releasing a pungent odor. Lekki was unmoved, but Rembly smiled, dumping its contents onto his desk. An audible rumble called from his stomach, and his mouth began to water.

Several large handfuls of pale blue mushrooms and bits of wet gravel fell onto the desk, with a few bulbous caps tumbling to the ground. Lekki bent to collect them and returned them to the table, smiling.

"I found these near the southern refinement station, but there were so many! More than I could fit inside the container. I've never seen a patch that large before," Lekki said, picking up a morsel and turning it between her fingers.

A parting gift from Paran, then. Rembly eyed the larger-than-normal harvest of mushrooms—his favorite.

"These are quite lovely specimens you've found. Have you finished er...documenting them?" Rembly asked, plucking the largest mushroom he could find in the lot from the table, admiring it beneath the light. "May I?"

"Yes, Confessor," Lekki looked away. Rembly lifted his mask over his nose, breathing in the bouquet of fresh fungi. He stuffed the mushroom into his mouth and began to chew, grabbing two additional morsels from the table and pressing them into his cheek cavities. Rembly folded down the hood and tapped on the table. He wiped his wet fingers on his robe, sinking deep into the blissful taste. The room echoed with sounds of his labored chewing and breathing beneath the mask.

Lekki turned back and grinned. "I know you like these, so I'll try and head out again tomorrow when the refinery pauses. I've been able to walk among the miners, and they don't seem bothered by my harvesting. Honestly, I'm not sure they notice me at all."

Rembly nodded, his taste buds dancing with delight as he nestled into Lekki's gentle voice. She foraged often for anything edible within the mines, a hobby turned obsession over the last few months. Rembly devoured the luscious and chewy mushrooms, reminiscing about how long Lekki had been his shadow since he'd rescued her from a local cult over a decade ago. "You," Rembly paused and swallowed the remaining mouthful. "You know how much I love your visits. Thank you for taking the time to sit with me so often."

Lekki smiled and took the canister back. She shut the lid and locked it, placing the container on the floor. "Yes, Confessor."

"I have always enjoyed your company, Lekki. You have grown so much since that first time I saw you crying alone in that wretched cult, lost and afraid," Rembly sighed, retrieving a canvas bag from the floor near his chair. He grunted, bending over. "I remember how scared you were. I was afraid, too. I'd never seen a child before I met you."

Lekki brushed a strand of hair behind her ear. "That was a long time ago. I've grown up a lot since you found me."

"Yes. Now look at you, braving the darkest corners of this dreadful mine to satiate your passionate curiosity." Rembly swiped the rest of the mushrooms into the open bag propped up in his lap. "A true gift lies within this passion of yours, my dear."

The swelling sadness in his heart pushed into his throat and escaped as a whimper. Rembly quieted himself, desperate to bottle up the emotion that dared to escape. It wouldn't hold much longer.

"I wanted to tell you, Confessor," Lekki broke the silence, "I flushed the carbon air filters outside your office and discovered why you weren't getting hot water in your apartment. It was due to a mineral build-up on the incomi—"

Rembly held up his hand. His brown palm was smeared with wet gravel and flecks of blue mushroom.

"You do too much for me," Rembly said. "May your gifts be *his*, not mine. Your gifts are many, and they will serve Paran well. Which reminds me..." Rembly looked down at the rings on the table and found himself unable to focus on anything but the fading scent and flavor from the mushrooms he'd eaten. The constant noise beyond the walls began to subside, indicating that a shift was changing in the mines.

"Yes, confessor?" Lekki began to fidget with a loose fiber on her glove.

Rembly took a deep breath and coughed some remnants of blue fungi into his mouth. It had been a long time since he'd eaten anything so fresh. Everyone in the mine received a standard nutrient-rich but flavorless chewable bark that arrived in large shipments every quarter. It was bitter and nothing like this luscious harvest, which had a profound and pleasant taste. He relished the gift, still singing on his tongue, and rubbed the bag in his lap.

"Lekki, there is something I must tell you," Rembly continued, placing his satchel on the floor. "A detachment from the Citadel of Paran will be coming soon, maybe even tonight, to pick you up and—"

"I've been selected?" Lekki jumped up from her stool, knocking it to the ground. She cheered, bouncing on her toes.

Rembly nodded. "I sent in your applications as requested, but it seems you have been chosen for something much more important than we could have imagined."

Lekki grabbed the edge of the desk in front of her, bracing against it. "What? What is it?"

"You have been selected to become the Holy Fixer of TAKER 7," Rembly said as calmly as he could muster, but his voice cracked at the tail end. His hands were clenched around the armrests again. "The second Holy Fixer ever to be chosen, it would seem. TAKER 5 was the last..." Rembly stopped. He struggled to continue. His hands were aching. "Congratulations."

"It can't be," Lekki said, her eyes wide, taking a step back. She stumbled and almost tripped over the stool. "I had no idea it was complete! I didn't even apply!"

"Please breathe and sit for a moment," Rembly said, knowing he could do nothing to help her from tumbling in his current state. "Sit and confess to me one last time. It will calm us both down, perhaps."

He needed to breathe and listen to her. Old fool. She was leaving, and there was nothing he could do about it. After all, he was the one who'd sent in her application. Was it all that surprising, considering how rare children are these days? Besides, there was no future for her here.

Lekki paused her mouth agape, and looked around. She closed her mouth and took several deep breaths before picking up the fallen stool from the floor. She spun on its uneven swivel to face Rembly.

The confessor began murmuring rote words of healing to himself, desperate to control the swelling grief that was overwhelming him. His paper-thin attempt to hold it back failed once he dared to look upon Lekki's thoughtful, tender eyes. They melted right through him.

"I'm losing the only child I've ever known," Rembly blurted out, tears now flowing behind his mask. "Why must so few of you exist in this world? What happens to this place when its light is gone? Confess to me now; how might I go on without you?"

Lekki took a deep breath and recited the Ritual of Peace.

"Paran has filled us all with the promise of peace, and we need only ask for it. Suffering, be it from a shattered soul or self-infliction or forces beyond our control, his power banishes all," Lekki said in a calm and confident tone. She traced the outline of Paran's Citadel Pyramid in the air. "All suffering is banished. Peace is his promise." She placed her arm over her shoulder and bowed.

His confession was genuine and heartfelt. Her response was perfect. Paran had chosen well.

Rembly sniffed aloud and dabbed his mask to his face. The fabric clung to his wet cheeks, sopping up the confessor's tears. "One last confession. Are you afraid? The TAKER must walk alone amid an endless sea of danger, ensuring the largest gifts for Paran's Empire to survive. So I ask again, are you afraid?"

He knew *he* was.

"I am not," Lekki said, lifting her head, a broad smile brimming with excitement. "Confessor, I cannot wait!"

A gift of youth. Fear would come with age.

"The confession is now complete. May your gifts be his." Rembly mumbled, mucus dripping from his nose around his thick mustache. He massaged his face with the mask, but it was becoming unbearable. "I need you to know I won't be able to join you, my dear."

Lekki's shoulders dropped, and she furrowed her eyebrows. "You can't? But I thought you were supposed to tutor me if I was chosen. Aren't I to have a mentor?"

"That was my hope, but Paran has other plans. Holy Fixers must have individualized training," Rembly said, his soiled mask sagging away from his face. The openings for his eyes and mouth drooped beneath where he needed them. He prodded at the fabric with both hands but soon gave up. He'd tear the thing from his face if it wouldn't constitute blasphemy. "My plans have also changed. Soon, I will partake in the Sacrament of Clarity. I will be free of my suffering."

Lekki shook her head. "No. I will request that you be stationed with me. They may let me—"

Rembly raised both hands this time and leaned forward, his ghoulish mask sagging and swaying. "No, it has already been decided. I have no choice in the matter. Now, please, my dear, go and collect your things. The envoy may arrive at any moment," he rasped.

Lekki hesitated but reached out for the confessor's hand. Rembly waved her away, unable to oblige. Tears were pooling in Lekki's eyes. She rose in silence to leave, tapping the door control panel. It opened, but she paused before leaving. "Thank you, confessor, for your teachings. For everything. I wish you were coming with me."

Rembly nodded, then jumped in his chair. Curling a finger in the air, he motioned for Lekki to return.

"Wait! I almost forgot I wanted you to have something of mine." Rembly scooped the satchel from the ground and opened it in his lap. He rummaged through the bag until he found the trinket, pulling it up and out of the crumpled mushrooms. Suspended from his clenched fist with a thin, tensile cord swung a small, obsidian prism. "Here, please come and take it from me."

Lekki took the rectangular object and held it under the light. "What is it? It's beautiful."

"My memory shard. Well, now it is your memory shard," Rembly said, closing up his satchel and tossing it to the floor. "It was given to me when I first became a confessor. It holds my truth. It keeps it safe. My life's work and journals reside within, some of which may shock you, especially regarding your former home. There are terminals in the city that will help you access what is contained inside and allow you to add your own truths to the shard."

The dark shard glistened between Lekki's fingertips. "Confessor, I..."

"May you remember me with this and," he squeaked, "make new memories of your own, my dear." Rembly sobbed, his ludicrous mask pushing him to the brink of blasphemy. He began shooing Lekki to leave despite everything within him begging her to stay. "Now, go! May your gifts be his."

"Thank you, Confessor," Lekki whispered, placing the lanyard around her neck and leaving. "I will miss you more than you know. May your gifts be his." She sniffed and wiped tears from her eyes.

The confessor silently screamed behind the soiled veil, unable to speak through his gaping mouth. Lekki lingered beyond the open doorway. Rembly considered running to her and embracing the child one last time. One final, warm embrace before they faded away from each other forever.

The automatic door slammed shut. Lekki was gone.

Rembly tore at the accursed mask, wailing, the wet cloth sloughing away from his face. Once free, he flung the wretched mask at the golden script upon the wall and collapsed into his crossed arms. Biting down hard on the loose fabric of his robes, Rembly began to scream.

The light in the room flickered as the machinery beyond the walls came alive again, drowning out his weeping with the abrasive thundering of copper ore being pulverized and smelted outside the subterranean office.

4 / KELS

REMARKABLY SIMILAR-LOOKING women packed a large boardroom, facing the one sporting gray silk. The clones were identical, differentiated by variations within their uniforms and how they wore their hair or makeup—if any. Kels surveyed the room, counting the number of her sisters arriving for the meeting. She stood near the exit, ready to act if called upon, a habit due to her specialization.

Kels's specialization revolved around her assignment. Like her sister Kay, she was assigned as one of Paran's aides. They both received extensive training in combat, medicine, and diplomacy. The difference between their specializations was that Kels was chosen to learn starcraft piloting while Kay was selected to learn counterintelligence.

Paran had replaced most, if not all, of his upper leadership with clones of his long-dead partner, also named Kels. The original was his most trusted advisor and confidant. She was a skilled researcher in pharmacology, so Paran had many of her clones trained in various research specializations.

The clones, however, were not treated like trusted advisors or confidants. They were treated like slaves and replaced as soon as they fell below a performance threshold or showed the slightest interest in freedom or resistance. Nevertheless, they were well-trained and equipped for various vital tasks to keep Paran's empire running smoothly.

Ironically, the counterintelligence training Kay received was how the sisters created the resistance network. She developed an entire system for relaying messages to other clones as far away as the moon. Recruiting was difficult to orchestrate, but no clone had ever denied an invitation.

The fact that it was being held within Paran's Citadel seemed suicidal, but Paran hadn't returned to the tower for months. Kels also knew the tower's layout and had high-level security clearance due to her assignment.

Another group of sisters entered wearing jumpsuits and coveralls. Kay sat at the head of the large conference table. After ensuring the hall outside was empty, Kels nodded, the two sharing a tense smile. Kay cleared her throat, and the room fell silent.

"Please come sit next to me," Kay said, motioning Kels to an empty chair to her right. "We are about to begin."

Kels sat next to her counterpart, and Kay touched a control panel on the desk. This shut the double doors and turned the windows around the boardroom opaque. The doors locked, a green light flipping to red on the handles.

"I'm disabling surveillance for this meeting. Security is

aware, and our sister who oversees that department has guaranteed this meeting will not be recorded." Kay tapped in a few more commands. The security system, indicated by a circular red ring above the conference room doors, faded away. "There. Now, let's begin."

Kels pushed her office chair away from the table, bumping into something. She apologized for bumping into one of her sisters, but the space behind her was empty. They must have moved.

An energetic hum permeated the silence.

"Thank you all for coming on such short notice. A serious matter requires our immediate attention," Kay asserted.

She gestured to a sister seated halfway down the massive conference table. The woman, who wore muted green coveralls and a grave expression, took a deep breath. "Sisters, thank you for meeting with me. I've come with news that will likely cause you great distress, but I hope we can..." she paused, her voice shaky. "We can find a way through this nightmare. We can find a way to help Rivir."

A collective gasp filled the room. Kay touched the console, and three nested rings—red, blue, and green—emerged from hidden compartments within the massive obsidian conference table. The rings glowed, and the warm overhead lights dimmed. Audio played from speakers hidden within the boardroom walls.

The hologram was yet another clone of Kels, dressed in green coveralls like the sister who delivered the message. The hologram was panting. Saucer eyes darted about, blood dripping beneath her nose. "Sisters... sisters... I don't have much time," she whispered. "It's about Rivir. I send this to you from the House of Eternity... where TAKER 7 has been completed."

Kels's mouth dropped agape in unison with several others in the room. Kay took her hand and squeezed it.

"TAKER 7 will not replace..." The image faltered. "This was a deception to keep us in the dark as...wait," the clone froze mid-sentence, silent. Audible footsteps came closer and faded away. She paused, her ear pressed against a panel wall before whispering. "TAKER 7 is going to Cora! It is intended to take what cannot be taken! Oh, my sisters, I discovered this only a few days ago and cannot keep it hidden from you any longer."

Kels's blood ran cold, and one of her sisters fainted. There were plans to rescue Rivir before the launch of TAKER 7. Rivir, the child of Paran and the original Kels, was defenseless and needed help. She looked to Kay for answers. Her sister nodded toward the hologram.

"I didn't have much time, but while overseeing the final safety protocols for all personnel within the titan, I managed to slip in a ritual to enable and disable TAKER 7. I disguised it as a minor ritual for..." The display went dark, the recording device obscured by the hologram's hand. "Since I am the one who approves the final ritual implementations, it has already been—"

A booming sound blared through the speakers, and Kels winced. The hologram wore a face of determined fury amid obsidian-armored hands clutching at her. "You will have to play a song, sisters! The ritual is a song! You know the song!" The recording stopped.

Kay retracted the holovid rings and turned the lights back on. She stood, pausing amid the shaken women whispering to one another. "Thank you for getting us this message, sister. I saw it for the first time yesterday, but the transmission is a few weeks old. As some of you may know, TAKER 7's Holy Pilot and Holy Fixer have already been selected. We have a limited time before—"

Kay's mouth snapped shut, her cheeks pressing inward in an unnatural shape. Her twisted lips held back a muffled scream, her body wrestling against invisible restraints. Kels approached her sister with caution.

An energetic hum permeated the silence.

"Now that the entertainment is over," seethed a cold, robotic voice behind Kay. The disembodied utterance took the form of a Black Thaumaturge emerging from thin air, an armored hand covering Kay's mouth. Brothers, the ritual of the hunt is yours to commence. You may begin."

Time slowed. The Thaumaturge retrieved a humming black dagger with their free hand. Kels recalled an encounter with these warriors during her combat training. They wore powerful armor and carried a transforming blade called a misericorde. This one had a single green dot near the center of their helmet.

The dagger plunged into Kay's back. "Die, traitor."

"No!" Kels gasped, the blade protruding from Kay's chest. The Black Thaumaturge withdrew her misericorde as the room erupted into chaos. Some of her sisters ducked beneath the table while others went for the locked doors, trying to force them open. Slumping onto the conference table, Kay shuddered, wheezing through a pierced lung.

The assassin stalked around the table opposite Kels, moving toward a group huddled together near the end of the conference room. Kay braced herself on the console for room controls. With a trembling red hand, she tapped the commands to open the doors, disable the window privacy screens, and re-enable security. "Get out of here!" Kay collapsed to the floor.

Kels rushed to her fallen sister, holding her hand and cradling her head. There was no chance of saving her life. She leaned close, many of her sisters flooding out of the boardroom amidst the screeching security alarms.

"You need to find a way," Kay coughed, her teeth red. "Get to security with as many as you..." Her voice trailed off, along with her gaze. She stopped moving. Kels closed her sister's eyes.

Adrenaline numbed the pain. Her breathing slowed. Her focus narrowed. Training took over. Kels wouldn't win in direct combat, but she might escape. She could escape with some of her sisters. She had to try. There still was a chance to save her child, Rivir.

"Was that a joke?" A harsh voice crackled from across the enormous conference table. At the far end of the boardroom, the Black Thaumaturge swung an obsidian sword, butchering one of her sisters who attempted to fight back. The assassin laughed. "Oh, Zeta, you're missing all the fun!"

Kels squeezed Kay's hand before slinking out of the boardroom and into the hall. A sister wearing a yellow jumpsuit—a security uniform—bolted toward her from the library. "Get to the service lift!" They shouted, scrambling around the droves fleeing the boardroom. "Get to the service lift!"

The service lift wasn't far, but many had scattered in the opposite direction. Kels called out to them, a few turning amidst the chaos. "Come with me! We're not far from the lift!"

Distant, terrified screams and the droning of various alarms were their escort along the way. When she reached the lift, several sisters were waiting inside. Not even half the number from the boardroom. She ushered her followers and a few remaining stragglers through the open elevator doors, addressing them all at once.

"The lift has only one destination: the basement," Kels barked into the compartment. "Security is stationed right outside where the doors open. I believe help will be waiting for you there. Good luck!" Without hesitation, she slapped a large red button, and the doors shut, closing on about twenty copies of herself staring wide-eyed back at her. The sound of the lift descending away from the violence gave Kels a moment of relief.

She ran back to the boardroom.

Kels found her yellow-clad sister pushing a large cabinet against the locked conference room doors. The ballistic shatter-proof windows were streaked with blood but not broken. Kels ducked alongside and helped shove the heavy cabinet against the doors.

A shattering above their heads startled them both. A web of fractured glass spread from where it had been struck, but the window did not break.

"Don't stop pushing," her sister said, wiping her brow. "But cover your ears!"

Kels did as instructed while the security specialist rolled up her right sleeve, exposing a control panel flush with her skin. After tapping the screen with two metallic fingertips, her sister winced, cupping her ears. A concussive blast from within the boardroom rocked the two sisters.

Jumping to her feet and sprinting toward the service lift, Kels's sister yelled, "Come on!"

Beyond the bloody glass windows, the boardroom teemed with dense, pillowy sludge—fire retardant. A lot of it. Kels practiced fire drills quarterly. Without fire to soften it, the gel would remain sticky until it dried out and crumbled. Ten minutes, give or take.

"What's your name?" Kels called out, running to catch up.

"Call me Sy." She glanced at the panel embedded in her forearm. "The lift is on its way back up, and our sisters are safe below, for now. If Alpha breaks out of that room before it arrives," Sy retrieved a heavy red ball from her cargo pocket and handed it to Kels. "Throw this directly at the Thaumaturge and find another way down. I'll meet you in docking bay nine once I've ensured none of our sisters are still hiding on this floor."

"Let me go with you. I have combat training," Kels said, lifting the ball to Sy. "What's this?"

"A grenade filled with the same stuff currently blanketing the conference room. It should hopefully buy you a few minutes, depending on where you hit. My counterpart said six of the Black Thaumaturges are in the Citadel, one clearing each floor starting from the top down...but according to my records, there should be seven of them." Sy mumbled, turning away. "Paran's issued a death warrant on us all. It's all over the official channels now. He's doing a complete purge and starting fresh."

As the sisters descended the hall, they stumbled upon the kitchen.

"Is anyone here?" Kels called out. "Sisters, if you're hiding, we must leave quickly." Kels looked around the deserted space. Like the boardroom, a floor-to-ceiling window dominated the room's far end.

In the corner, black marble countertops created a half-circle prep area. A vase of fresh roses filled the space with a delicate aroma. Refrigerators hummed against the walls. A wooden bowl sat on the dining room table, brimming with fresh fruit, the rare delicacies brought daily from the hydroponic gardens below. Waste like this was a common frequency at such heights in the Citadel.

A clinking sound came from behind the prep area. Sy inched toward the sound, raising a red ball in the air. A sister wearing a white lab coat rose from behind the countertop. "Is it safe to come out?" she asked, gripping a quivering kitchen knife.

"Not really, but you're dead if you stay here." Sy waved her sister out. "Is anyone with you?"

"No, I haven't heard anyone come this way since..." She trailed off, shaking her head.

Sy glanced at her arm. "We need to go," she made for the door and checked the hallway. "What should we call you? You're from off-world, right?"

"Kel—ah, Doc is fine," she shrugged. "I'm not used to being around this many versions of me, of us."

Sy winked. "We can come up with new names once we get out of the Citadel."

The three rushed to the service elevator, the doors opening as they arrived. The lift was empty, and Kels waited until her sisters boarded before stepping in. Looking back toward the end of the hall, she noticed a shift in the hallway. Instinctively, she lurched back into the elevator, dodging a spear that shot past the open lift doors.

Kels glanced back into the hallway. A stumbling prism approached, bits of white foam drifting off the phantom. Kels squeezed the ball of fire retardant.

Without hesitation, she stepped out of the lift and threw it. Thick gel and foam exploded around the Thaumaturge's concealed appendages. The warrior stumbled, still down the hall, swiping at the slime covering its body. The frothing prism turned obsidian, struggling to remove the hazy slime from its visor.

Kels ducked back into the elevator, raising a finger to Sy. "Can you disable power to the VIP lift for this floor?"

Sy nodded, her expression a mix of confusion and concern.

"Do it."

"What are you—?" Sy hissed, but Kels had already moved back into the hallway.

Kels spotted the VIP lift she took daily from Paran's living quarters at the top of the Citadel. The shaft ran hundreds of floors down to the lobby. She retrieved the spear from the wall and pried open the disabled elevator doors.

"Zeta! Where the hell are you!?" The Thaumaturge roared, smearing the murky gel about their visor.

Kels answered the question with a spear. The thrust didn't pierce the assassin's armor, but the stunned Thaumaturge staggered back, slipping on the gel. Kels tossed the spear toward the VIP lift.

Grabbing an armored foot, Kels dragged the assassin

through the muck toward the open shaft. She stopped at the edge to pick up the spear, the dazed Thaumaturge struggling to regain its footing. Kels stabbed again at the warrior. The blow knocked them halfway past the threshold.

The Thaumaturge grabbed the door before falling, pulling itself back into the hallway. The ventilation from the open shaft fanned the fire retardant, causing it to crumble away from their visor.

The assassin snarled. "Give me that!"

Kels thrust at their head again. The Thaumaturge caught the spear with both hands, but Kels followed through with a strong side kick to their torso. The decisive blow sent the assassin over the edge.

The decrescendo of the Thaumaturge slamming against the shaft walls reverberated into the hallway, then stopped. Deep inside the abyss, a traction cable jerked away from the wall and went taught. It was coming back. Kels followed the cable taught to the lift several stories above her.

"Sy, disable the magnets that secure the VIP lift!"

A loud buzzing alarm forced Kels to cover her ears. Ten tons of vacant VIP lift plummeted past her, and a gust of wind knocked her to the ground.

"There," Kels dusted off her navy trousers. "Hopefully, that will be enough."

"I didn't know you were a combat specialist," Sy said once the doors to the service lift closed. Her eyes were wide. "That's not in your dossier."

"Kay and I both were," Kels said, checking for any wounds. "Although we were never trained to fight against Thaumaturges," she closed her eyes and shook her head. "I'm also a pilot specialist if that helps."

"Listen," Sy announced. "There's a cloaked ship in the basement waiting for us, and it's our only way to safety right now. Once you step inside, there's no coming back. We are going off-world until we devise a plan to rescue Rivir. If you stay here, you *will* die."

Kels closed her eyes and nodded; sudden pangs of loss and guilt crept into her mind. She leaned on her training to stay calm. There would be time for tears later.

"I'm coming with you," Kels said, opening her eyes. Doc crouched in the corner, still gripping the kitchen knife.

"The song..." Doc stood up. "It's what we played for River as they fell asleep, right?"

Kels and Sy nodded, and Doc laughed. "Isn't it strange to know something like that, especially since I've never played a kana flute, much less rocked a baby to sleep? I've never even seen one. Yet I hold those memories dearly for a child that isn't mine." Doc, her eyes now glistening with tears, dropped the knife. "Do you think we can help Rivir? I'd do anything..."

"We have a plan," Sy said. "And help."

Doc hesitated, then nodded, wiping her eyes. "Okay then, I'm with you." The sisters descended in silence until the lift stopped at the basement.

Kels followed her sisters into docking bay nine through a shimmering silver portal. Inside, the rest of her surviving sisters huddled together in a half-empty cargo hold about twice the size of the boardroom.

"You're all here," Kels whispered, relieved. Their faces radiated determination and concern—concern for Rivir. Kels would go to any lengths to save her child, and her sisters likely felt the same, each in their own way. Despite their differences in assignment and appearance, each clone shared several intrinsic truths, with the imperative to keep Rivir safe rising above all else.

No amount of indoctrination could sever that connection. Not for them.

"How are we getting out of here?" Doc asked, the portal closing behind them.

Sy clapped her hands and shouted. "Listen up!"

The crowd paused and moved to give Sy some space, forming a circle around her.

"An Orbit Crawler is on its way to pick us up. It will take us to the spaceport just outside the planet's surface. From there, we will uncloak and drop into the Voidstream. Kels—" Sy pointed, and the crowd parted in confusion until Kels touched her chest, with Sy nodding. "Kels is a pilot specialist and will guide us through the Voidstream to our next destination."

Kels swallowed hard at the announcement. She had practiced Voidstream flight in a simulator, not an actual starcraft. She glanced around the cargo bay's interior and realized she didn't recognize anything about the alien vessel. Sy winked at her before continuing.

"On that note, think of a new name for yourselves since we can't all go by the name Kels. Even if we can easily tell each other apart, it will get too confusing when we're all together like this," Sy smirked, adjusting her collar. "Call me Sy, by the way."

Kels closed her eyes; memories of laughing with Kay over

coffee earlier in the week forced their way in. The adrenaline was wearing off; she'd crash hard soon.

"We're going to meet a contact in deep space who is connected to a group called The Integration." Sy let the announcement hang in the air for a moment. While some of her sisters reacted in shock, most remained silent. "A few of you may have heard whispers about this organization, but they aren't rumors. They exist beyond Paran's reach, and this ship can help us get there. I won't lie. Humans aren't usually welcome, but their leadership has made an exception for us. They understand our motivations, and we hold great value for them because we are, well, so intimately familiar with Paran." Sy paused, gauging the mood in the room.

Several of the sisters began to cry. Kels didn't quite grasp everything Sy had said, but she assumed it meant that wherever they were going involved leaving everything behind. For Kels, that was easy, as she had led an isolated life with little company besides Kay and, sporadically, Paran. However, many of her sisters had deep community ties to the megacities' dwindling population, which decreased yearly due to the alarmingly low birth rate.

"We're not just doing this for Rivir," Sy continued. "The Integration wants to help us save our planet, too. They understand that we are prisoners under Paran and want to help us break free. If you don't want to join the fight, you don't have to. My contact promised safe passage to a human community within The Integration that isn't involved in the war effort, but you're no longer safe here."

A massive, blaring dock alarm rang so loud that it rattled the cloaked starcraft, and one of the sisters called out from the edge of the group, "That's the Orbit Crawler. It's here!"

The ship began to wobble, a familiar experience from the simulations. Her legs remained steady despite the turbulence.

The Orbit Crawler docked and collected the empty-looking freight container, charging its reactor before uncoupling from the dock and falling back in line with several others. All were heading in the same direction, drifting deep into the cloudless night sky.

Kels wiped the sweat from her forehead, recalling her pilot simulation training. Her exhaustion was catching up to her. She paced the cargo bay, half smiling at her sisters—so many had been taken before their journey had even begun.

When she thought of Rivir, the chaos in her mind melted away. She paused, took a deep breath, and closed her eyes. A hand on her shoulder opened them back up.

"Let me show you to the cockpit," Sy said, her smile widening. "Captain."

GLOWING tips of incense offered fragrant tendrils of soft smoke to the woman standing before the altar. Morna took a deep breath, the aromatics dancing about her face. After several breaths, she found herself in a peaceful calm and opened her eyes.

A modest platform with small stones and wood tokens strewn about the surface. Near the back of the table, incense smoldered in a clay saucer. Small candles illuminated the space, and shadows danced with the tiny flames flickering on their wicks. A sturdy wooden box lay in the center. She paused her breathing.

"Oh, Butterfly."

The small box was hand carved and hand painted; a thin, elongated body of a whimsical creature flanked by oversized, colorful wings adorned the lid. An ornate golden twine wrapped around the red wings held the case shut, threaded together through a brass coin.

Morna smiled, reaching down to scoop the box off the altar. She paused, holding something in her hand. Before lifting the box, she set her well-worn misericord on the altar.

She rocked the artisanal box, clutching it gently near her abdomen where the contents once grew. It had been years since her miscarriage, but the dull ache of grief remained. She brought the wooden butterfly to her lips and kissed it softly before returning it to the altar. She offered a prayer in silence before gathering her blade and snuffing out the incense and candles.

"Lights," she said into the pitch-black room. An orb in the ceiling cast harsh light about her, and squinting, she reached for her helmet. She affixed the Misericorde to her waist and lifted the obsidian helm, glancing at her reflection in the visor.

Brown eyes surrounded by russet brown skin gazed back, her braids tight against her scalp. Morna slipped the helmet on. A single red dot glowed in the visor before her eyes, moving up and out of sight while lens filters and sensors initialized.

A message alert blinked in the corner of her visor. With her eyes fixated on it and a swipe of her armored thumb and index finger, the message replayed.

"Hey, beautiful, it's me," Benny said softly with his brassy voice. "Lekki and I just finished breakfast. Can you believe she's never had pancakes? I was hoping to save you some, but..."

Morna smiled. Benny was quite proud of his pancakes. He should be.

"Come on down when you can. I'd love for you to try to meet her before she leaves. I can't believe it's been six months already." Benny's voice diminished to a whisper. "Just make sure you're wearing your helmet. She was raised by some looney confessor who'd been locked away in a copper mine, so she's... well, just wear your helmet. She's afraid her face will melt off if she looks at you, saying it's blasphemy. Paran's done a number on this one." Lekki appeared behind him in the message, and Benny turned red. "Anyway, hope to see you soon. Kisses."

Morna's smile faded. She closed the message from her partner. It had been sent hours ago while Morna was still piloting TAKER 5, awaiting rendezvous coordinates for Lekki's departure. TAKER 7 would be heading to Cora soon, and Lekki had been learning the fundamentals of being a Holy Fixer alongside Benny, who was the first. It was ridiculous to think Lekki would be ready for such a mission with so little training, yet that was the timeline.

Piloting a TAKER was exhausting yet exhilarating. Each pilot had a somewhat different apparatus to sync themselves with the titans, Morna's being similar to TAKER 7's pilot, Djonah. Inside its gargantuan head, the Holy Pilot was encased within a second suit of armor surrounded by a myriad metallic nodules. It was cumbersome yet comfortable. Within a massive dome filled with various ferrofluids and coolants, superconducting magnet sensors lining the dome walls held the pilot in place. The pilot's movements were captured in real-time, and the TAKER mimicked every move.

Morna walked through the door from her bedroom into a large foyer. The walls within the foyer were filled with murals of staggering proportions, with a single door beneath each masterpiece. One of the four previous TAKERS adorned each of the four walls. They were stylized with soft edges and standing in gentle poses, surrounded by colorful flowers and dancing children. She stopped and took in the image of TAKER 1, standing over a flourishing megacity, guarding Paran's Citadel. The pyramid at the top shimmered with pyrite.

The blinking red notification inside her helmet broke Morna's attention, and she went through the black door beneath TAKER 2. As she approached, the door slid beneath the floor. The room beyond was a small, featureless chamber similar to her bedroom. A medical recovery pod and hypersleep chamber stood on one side, a circular platform on the other. Fixing on the platform, a smile returned. Benny waited below.

On the platform, Morna gradually sank beneath the floor until she was swallowed whole. She descended through a dark tunnel lined with a mucosal membrane protected by her armor. The organic passage was endless, Morna replaying Benny's message several times until she lowered from the ceiling of another chamber. The platform came to rest in a sprawling industrial warehouse, teeming with grids of supply containers.

"I was wondering when you'd finally show up!"

Benny, whose cheeks and balding head were the same color as his red ARC Repair suit, wore a much larger, more utilitarian version of Morna's armor. He slurped at a glass of milk, leaving a dripping white line along his bristly red mustache. His armored gauntlets were three times the size of Morna's, the cup in his hands appearing as small as a vial. He offered the glass to Morna.

She shook her head. "I'd rather have a coffee."

"Right this way, your highness." Benny feigned offense before finishing the glass of milk and heading down the sprawling warehouse toward his workshop. "Lekki's already gone, by the way."

"I know." Morna reached for Benny's hand, catching up to him. "Are you upset with me?"

Benny shrugged. "Maybe it was for the best. She was terrified of you, despite my best efforts to explain to her that you were not some angel of death—" Benny paused, his turning a brighter shade of red.

"She knows I am a Holy Pilot, and I'm sure she read the reports on both of us before coming aboard. She knew I was the previous Alpha of the Black Thaumaturges, and she likely feared the consequences of blasphemy for looking upon the face of a Holy Pilot. I don't blame her."

Benny let out a booming laugh, echoing throughout the colossal warehouse. "Holy Pilot, eh? Black Thaumaturge, eh? Where are the reports regarding you being an incredible kisser? What say the Holy Decrees regarding your angelic voice?"

Morna stopped, putting her hands on her hips. "Yes, where are those documents? I would love to see them myself." She tried to hide the smile in her reply. She fell back into holding his hand, squeezing it tight.

The vast storage facility contained tens of thousands of industrial supply containers, looming over the lovers on either side of the passageway. The hum of distant machinery whirred from some unseen place within the TAKER. It wasn't so alien any longer. It was home.

When they reached Benny's workshop, Morna pressed her hand to the console along the entrance. The reinforced bulkhead door responded by gliding horizontally into the wall to her right. Benny's workshop wasn't as cavernous as the storage facility but dwarfed Morna's living quarters. The clutter inside was, as usual, off-putting, but the aromas of cooked bacon and fresh, hot coffee pushed her feelings aside.

Benny's kitchenette and dining table were at the far end of the room, beckoning. Above, the mesh weave net hanging high in the workshop shimmered in diffuse light. Morna's mouth watered. The coffee carafe stood out among the remnants of a bountiful breakfast. Filling a mug with piping-hot coffee, she removed her helmet and relished the aroma. The dark roast was bitter. It was perfect.

"There's plenty left, so help yourself." Benny lumbered behind. "Lekki ate most of the bacon, though. I can't blame her."

The colors of the workshop were deep red and charcoal, alien runes and markings reminding Morna much of her existence was due to so much she couldn't comprehend. Glancing at her arm mid-sip, her form-fitted ebony armor reinforced the mystery. The suit was as much a secret to her as the TAKER itself. The armor enhanced her deadly skills in ways she couldn't fathom and was forbidden to do so anyway. Blasphemy.

Morna often pondered the suits worn by her and the other Thaumaturges. They were developed secretly, like the TAKERS themselves, shrouded in a veil of deception and ritual. Morna had been the first Thaumaturge to become a pilot and had hoped the promotion would bring her answers to the many burning questions that occupied her mind during her time as a soldier. Years later, she figured her curious nature had led to her selection as a pilot—now constrained by her inability to leave.

Benny tossed a pancake into the air and attempted to catch it on a plate. It flopped on the ground. She put a hand to her chest, laughing. At least she was trapped in here with him.

"How were the final days of Lekki's training?"

"Wonderful," Benny said, tossing a chunk of softened butter into the skillet. "She's great with a repair kit, but I believe her real talent is in research," he chuckled, scratching his chin with an oversized metal gauntlet. "Something I'm not so well-versed in, I regret to say."

"What about her ARC Suit?"

"What did she name it...? Benny smiled, tapping his chin. "Archie. I taught her all the basics. We spent most of the time reviewing basic repair, diagnostics, and triage. She spent most evenings behind the visor, studying the logs from a memory shard given to her by that confessor who raised her. I also let her copy all the data I've ever logged."

"And combat mode?" Morna took another sip of coffee, then grabbed a fork and jabbed at some of the thawed berries in a steel bowl.

Benny plated a few pancakes. "She knows the words. We practiced the proper rituals if she ever encountered a combatant." He turned the gas burner off and set the plate in front of Morna.

"Thank you." Morna spooned a few berries onto the pancakes, and Benny followed up with a splash of golden syrup. "I hope she never has to," she said, resting on the corner of the bench seat near the table. "She performed well in the fixer pod during the live piloting sessions. Hopefully, her pilot is as gifted as she is."

"Do you see who her pilot is?"

Morna nodded. "Djonah?"

"Poor kid, I read all about his upbringing. I still can't believe it. Honestly, Paran has changed so many rules since we left. I worry he's—"

Morna jerked her head sharp to the side at Benny, code for him to stop speaking. Paran had become less and less forgiving over the years, and Benny had already been close to being forced into the Sacrament of Clarity, the same ritual most of the remaining population had already participated in—rendering them mindless drones reliant upon a daily serum that removed all emotion from the mind.

She couldn't imagine Benny going through that.

"Are you so eager to participate in the Sacrament of Clarity, my love?" Morna mocked.

His toothy grin forced her smile to return. She lifted a cold slice of bacon into her mouth, the greasy delight making her quiver. She handed the last bite to the cook.

Benny shook his head. "Any word on our carrier arriving to take us along to Cora?"

Morna shrugged. "Paran is in a desperate situation. I imagine we will arrive at the same time TAKER 7 does. Although I don't know...with Lekki being on board, maybe Paran would send one of our other..." Morna stopped herself, unable to stomach the name she was supposed to call the other pilots.

"Our children..." Benny finished for her, a frown on his face. "The planet of Paran will be completely dead in a few decades, yet he keeps wasting resources on building pointless defenses. Enough talk. Enjoy your breakfast."

A prismatic purple light pulsated from underneath Benny's console, flashing in an otherwise dark corner of the workshop. Benny leaped up and ran straight toward the light.

"What is...that?" Morna said aloud, confused by the strange alert. She'd never seen anything like it before. "Is this something you created?"

"Maybe," Benny said almost defensively but then turned his head and winked at Morna. "It's a pirate radio if I had to give it a name. I can pick up transmissions that aren't moving through official channels. Don't worry, Paran can't see what I'm doing."

Morna was shocked yet not surprised. "This is... blasphemy," Morna whispered. "If Paran discovers you've built this—"

"What? He'll do what?" Benny scoffed, reaching the console. The Holy Fixer flipped down the helmet and visor of his ARC suit and retrieved a cable from its side, tethering the cord to a socket alongside the terminal. "He's mad, and you know it. I'm not pretending anymore. You don't have to either."

Benny pressed a few buttons on the foldout keypad, gesturing with his free hand to interact with whatever was displayed inside his red visor.

"What are you doing?" Morna asked, craning her neck to see the console screen scrolling with unfamiliar code and iconography.

"I'm trying to tether to the transmission. " He paused, then pressed a button to activate a small loudspeaker encased within the console. "Here we go."

A hissing sound seethed from the loudspeaker, followed by the distant voice of a man. It sounded faint and hollow as if the speaker were in a cave. Benny moved his free hand again, causing the voice to come in much clearer. Benny gave a thumbs up. "Should sound better now."

The voice spoke much louder as well, startling Benny. "Clones of Kels have been deemed blasphemy. I heard they sent the Black Thaumaturges to hunt them all down." The voice said, and Benny gasped at Morna, his mouth agape below the opaque visor he still wore. Morna shrugged, and the voice continued. "It seems a small group of them escaped with our rogue security specialist, who had already squirreled away some small improvised weapons, tools, even musical instruments with them. They hid away in one of the super loaders that—" The voice stopped and went silent.

"This voice," Benny said. "This voice, the transmission is coming from Paran. I can't tell where it's going, though."

"So it has some kind of AI on board?" The voice said. "They will need it if TAKER 7 is being sent to Cora. I wonder if the pilot and fixer will even survive that journey. It's anyone's guess what that amount of hypersleep will do to their memory."

The blood drained from Morna's face. She'd not considered the effects of extended hypersleep.

"Good to know," the voice said. "A tether frequency from where? Ah, that's TAKER 5. Didn't know they could listen in. Hello, TAKER 5."

"Ahhh!" Benny yelped, the speaker blurted out high-pitched squelching, and he tapped a few buttons on the console to end their tether. "Damn, what the hell was that?" Benny flipped his visor up and stared at his partner.

Morna stood for a moment in quiet contemplation. "Can you open that tether frequency to allow incoming communication?"

Benny nodded, "Well, sure, but that would alert Paran as—"

"Do it."

"So blasphemy is fine when you do it?" Benny grumbled, tapping at the console. He flipped his helmet down again and gestured with a finger, falling back into the data within his visor. Soon, the speaker was crackling again with a hiss and then silence. The silence was interrupted by a sudden, repetitive tone, and Benny went stiff.

"What is it?" Morna asked, touching Benny's shoulder and coaxing him toward her. "What is it, love?"

"Incoming transmission," Benny swallowed hard. "From deep space. The Integration."

"Open the line," Morna said, nodding to Benny. He nodded back and activated the comms.

"Hello, Morna. Hello, Benny lad," a jovial voice came from the other side of the line.

Morna did a double take at the familiar candor. "C... Crumb? Is that you?"

"Aww...you remember little old me?" Crumb said through the comm system, his creaky voice shrill over the speaker. "I'm chuffed!"

Benny furrowed his brow. "What is going on? Who's Crumb?"

"Happy to answer any and all questions, Benny boy, but time is of the essence, I'm afraid," Crumb said. Benny's wide-eyed expression turned to Morna, who shrugged. "I know you might have overheard, but TAKER 7 is heading for Cora, and The Integration is already preparing for its arrival. We can't let Paran continue playing his little game any longer. Cora is the last hope for everyone. It's the last habitable planet anywhere close that can sustain life. We need your support if we're gonna stop this madness once and for all."

Morna crossed her arms; memories of trading blows with Crumb before he escaped and fled beyond Paran's reach were creeping back into her mind. He had done lots of deep space reconnaissance work for Paran, even destroying remote outposts belonging to The Integration. One day, he switched sides, and Morna shuddered. Memories of the flash bomb he used on her to mask his escape flooded her mind.

"You're suggesting we trust you, a turncoat?" Morna snapped, getting strange glares from Benny.

"The Integration desperately needs people like me," Crumb replied. "I still get plenty of work, *and* I still get to visit plenty of beautiful places. Paran is a dead end. You both know this."

Benny nodded. "He's right about that, at least."

"Glad you agree, Benny boy," Crumb replied, Benny's smile turning upside down at the comment. "Listen, a carrier is cloaked in orbit to retrieve the both of you and bring you to Cora as soon as possible. We're hoping to have you arrive before TAKER 7, but it will be close."

"What about Lekki? And Djonah?" Benny said, leaning in close to the console. "I'm not hurting them."

"It seems like there is a way to disable TAKER 7, according to a group of defectors who arrived recently. They have a private message for you that I've sent your way on this...pirate radio, so you should be able to view it within the console after our conversation is over," Crumb said. "I don't believe The Integration wants them hurt either. Well, the leadership doesn't anyway."

The lovers gazed at each other. "We need to discuss this," Morna said. "How much time do we have to decide?"

"The carrier will leave tomorrow either way, although it will leave immediately if you send any transmissions before responding to me," Crumb replied. "So, I'd decide quickly. If you join us, I can promise safe passage on my ship once all this is over. Take you both wherever you want to go to start over. That is unless you both enjoy faffing about inside that walking mountain of yours?"

"Who's the private message from?" Benny asked, scrutinizing the console.

"Got to run, I'm afraid. Hope you both make the right decision," Crumb replied. "I've got a good feeling I'll see both real soon."

Crumb's connection ended and was replaced with an overpowering screech of digital static. Benny moved his hand, and the sound dropped away. He flipped his visor up to look at Morna. "The message is from Kels, and the origin signal is from Cora!"

"Let's chat before we listen to it." Morna went back toward Benny's dining table. It was still strewn with plates of half-eaten cold pancakes and bowls of berries from Benny's hydroponic garden. Thick slices of sourdough rested in a wicker basket. An empty dish lay smattered with sausage grease. She reached for a slice of bread. "I don't care what the message from Kels says," Morna said with her mouth full, "I want to go."

Benny took a seat at the table. "Are you sure?" He reached for an insulated carafe of coffee and refilled his cup until it was brimming with hot liquid. The scent caught Morna's attention, and she smiled. Benny reached for a clean mug from a stack near the table's end, filling it for her. "Isn't that just a tiny bit of blasphemy?"

"I joined Paran originally because I believed he would save our planet. Over a decade as a dedicated soldier. A handful as a Black Thaumaturge. Now, almost a hundred as a pilot, most of the time spent in hypersleep or roaming some desecrated planet," Morna said, pulling the coffee up to her lips, lingering in the comforting warmth. "I've been too late to realize that Paran is only going to save himself, and my concern at this point lies in the safety of the other pilots. I want to fight for them, for Lekki. I want to fight for the people of Paran." She took a sip.

Benny gulped his coffee. "He's on the offensive now with this move to take Cora. He always wanted the TAKERS to act as his primary invasion force."

"It's wrong," Morna frowned. "This technology wasn't meant for him to abuse it. I refuse to believe it."

"Who knows what this technology was meant for? Humans use it for whatever they want. That is its purpose."

Morna set her mug down. "You and I both know I'm right. This technology we wear as armor was meant to help us explore the universe, not to exploit it!" She closed her eyes and took a deep breath. Benny sipped his coffee, and the two sat until Morna opened her eyes. "Anyway, let's go listen to that message."

Morna picked up her coffee and followed Benny toward the console. She took a few sips along the way, taking in more of the messy workshop. The cavernous space echoed with the deep, muddled noises of the strange behemoth. The concert of alien bodily sounds intersected with manufactured systems, keeping both she and Benny alive and able to manipulate TAKER 5.

The titan was resting now, unable to move without Morna performing the ritual of piloting. Benny had long abandoned the ritual, but she didn't blame him.

Catching up to Benny, who was lost in his visor, she laid her head on his oversized armored shoulder.

"Oh, hey," he said, then smiled and put an arm around her. "I love it when you sneak up on me."

Morna sighed, closing her eyes and drifting in the comfort of his big arms for a moment. "More of this, please. Maybe even without the armor."

Benny laughed. "My door is always open," he said, releasing the hug. "I've loaded up the message from Kels. Are you ready?"

Morna nodded. She took another sip of coffee and found Benny reaching for her hand. She took it.

Benny flipped down his visor and then, with his free hand, pressed a button on the well-worn console. A flat metal platform ejected from a slot underneath the console's monitor, containing three nested, colorful rings. Benny and Morna stepped back as a projection formed before them, and a hologram of Kels appeared.

Morna's armored hand drifted from Benny to the soft curve of her stomach, where her dreams once grew.

Kels held a wind instrument—a kana flute. Before her miscarriage, a clone of Kels used to play songs for her with one of these, and she wondered if this was the same one.

"Hello, old friend," Kels said. "Hello, Benny. I've heard so much about you." She was wearing an upscale business suit and what appeared to be a spaceflight vest. "I'm hoping this finds you well."

Leaning over to Morna, Benny whispered, "I'm guessing you two also know each other?"

Morna pointed at the instrument. "She used to play such sweet music for me. Considering the consequences, none of the other clones I worked with dared. I'll never forget that."

Benny put an arm around her.

"Paran has to be stopped. He sent the Black Thaumaturges to kill my sisters. I don't know how many of us are left. I'm safe, for now, with The Integration, and they have plans to protect Cora and save the pilots and TAKERS themselves," she said. "That includes you. That includes TAKER 5."

Morna didn't react, but Benny let out a single dry laugh. She shushed her partner.

"Morna, I remember you as a caring mother who wanted nothing more than to help mold a better future for your child, and even when that dream couldn't be, you took up the responsibility of becoming the pilot of TAKER 5 along with Benny, guardian, and healer of all TAKERS. I ask you to join us in Cora to prepare for the arrival of TAKER 7. I believe I can turn them away from Paran."

Benny rolled his eyes. "She clearly hasn't met Lekki."

"I assume you don't know this, but an AI program is built inside TAKER 7. It is called Temple. It will monitor Djonah and Lekki and keep them safe," Kels said, a tear running down her cheek. "We didn't find out until it was too late, but additional protocols have been installed alongside Temple that will force the AI to kill Lekki and Djonah if they somehow stray from their mission."

Morna finished her coffee. Tiny grounds coated her tongue with bitterness. Benny reached back out for her hand, and she took it.

"This," Kels lifted her kana flute, "Might help us deactivate those deadly protocols within Temple and return them to..." her voice drifted, and a hand appeared from outside the projection to rub her shoulder. "Thanks," she whispered to someone out of view. "If we can deactivate these protocols, we can rescue the pilot and the fixer. If you're willing to join us, please consider contacting Crumb. The Integration has plenty of resources to help us reprogram and repair Temple. We can save Cora. We can save our people, too. Thank you."

The hologram smiled and disappeared, and Benny lifted his visor, reaching out for her other hand. She took in his relentless gray eyes. They were focused on her and wet around the sides. His bristly chin trembled. Benny sniffed. "Well, my love," he whispered. What do you think?"

Morna closed her eyes. "I need a moment," she said, squeezing Benny's hands. She went inward. This would mean breaking her ties with everything she had ever known, throwing away a lifetime of service to Paran for nothing but a certain death. Yet, the hope of saving Lekki and Djonah brought back a purpose she had almost forgotten. Stricken with rage and hope, she hadn't noticed she was crushing Benny's hands in her grip.

Benny grumbled. "I'm with you, either way, my love. I know how much—"

Morna opened her eyes, causing Benny to stop mid-sentence.

"Heavens, you're beautiful," Benny cooed, leaning in for a kiss.

Morna drank in the soft kiss and pulled him closer. They embraced in the darkness of the massive workshop. The heat from Benny's touch warmed through her armor, melting away the remnants of anger. She fell into him, letting his embrace anchor her. Morna slowly, begrudgingly, pulled herself away from lingering on his lips, gazing into her partner's stormcloud eyes.

"Let's get Crumb back on the line," she said. "Let's go to Cora."

SHIMMERING scarlet beads of light danced across the lavender twilight far above Cora. The playful movement distracted Gund from their quarry, and they set down their banruu on a patch of blue moss to enjoy the light show. The tiny dots resembled their patriarch, Chaxo, who several seasons ago stepped inside one of those strange starcraft and never returned.

Chaxo had allied with The Integration, an alien horde claiming it wanted to protect Cora from an inevitable threat. In the stars above, they would work together on a defense strategy, and Chaxo was the only adult Coran willing to leave the Red Mountains. Gund had pleaded to go along but was forbidden since they were still an adolescent.

Unfortunately, the threat arrived before any defenses could be put in place. During the previous rainy season, a monstrous dark egg fell from the sky west of the Red Mountains. Its impact quaked the land so much that Gund worried the world might split. The quaking subsided, and days later, a titan crawled out of the crater, shrieking from an unseen mouth.

It immediately set to violence, pulverizing the highest peak of the nearby mountain range and casting red stone debris in all directions. All of this unfolded from their tower, far away from the chaos.

The Red Mountains were sacred, as they were the home of Gund and their bond. The bond resided within a deep network of tunnels, now acting as a safe refuge from the invader. Gund had left the mountains a season before the calamitous monster arrived, seeking glory and purpose in the vast rainforests below.

It was the duty of each young Coran to perform this ritual before initiation into adulthood, and with initiation came assignment within the bond. The assignment was random and would remain for life. This journey was their last taste of freedom.

It was now the dry season, and Gund had been meditating in their tower for the last several nights while the massive titan with seven fervent eyes stood dormant, its immense hands caked in dust and blood. The alien beast had slain the dragon Voraxun, who guarded the Red Mountains. Its twisted carmine carcass was still draped along a crumbling mountain slope.

Gund witnessed the short battle and decided this titan's downfall would more than secure their place within their bond. This monster would become Gund's most incredible story, even if they failed. It was their purpose.

Then, they would join Chaxo or die. Either outcome was preferable to completing the initiation.

The small landing Gund stood upon connected to a pod, one of many in the twisted stone tower rising above the sprawling rainforest below. The towers were created ages ago, with some stories saying the dragons themselves had carved them out of a mountain range that used to reside here. Each tower was different, some larger than others, but each was tended to by the Corans, who used the spires as a precious refuge during their seasons in the brutal rainforest.

It kept all predators at bay for some reason, and even Voraxun had paid the towers no mind other than using them as a perch at times. Gund had taken great care to clean the space, replenish the cooking fuel, and leave behind a large wooden chair they'd carved out of a massive log they'd carried up to the pod. It would suffice as their contribution, satisfied it would be large enough for the next Coran from their bond to relax in, as they were larger than most.

Despite their seasons in the jungle, Gund encountered one other during their journey: a flying Coran named Hessu. Hessu was muted gold in color, slender, and had oversized wings. Hessu was vastly different in size and shape from the mountain dweller.

Even with their small frame, Hessu had a powerful singing voice. Their throat shone bright red, ballooning with air. Bending their banruu's strings to mimic their voice, Gund couldn't help but laugh. Hessu's eyes bulged with delight. The music was strange and familiar, and they both fell into laughter once the song finished. Gund found it hard to believe Corans like Hessu were revered as fearsome warriors, yet gruesome teeth emerged from their fleshy gums whenever they struck a high note in their song.

Hessu was kind and shared some dense and delightful

berries with Gund, keeping them sated for days. In return, Gund tended to a small tear in one of Hessu's wings. Hessu was returning south but was considering a jaunt along the market road to visit the new city before reuniting with their bond. They had asked Gund about their journey, but Gund had nothing to say. The question lingered long after Hessu had departed, along with the memory of Hessu's look of concern.

A journey was meant to last one season, and Gund had already been gone for two. They'd taken their banruu and a few precious trinkets, as the original plan had been to join their patriarch and find purpose among the stars, leaving Cora and the initiation behind. Chaxo had instructed Gund before he went to hold onto a communication device given to their bond by The Integration so Chaxo could send updates. Still, updates never came, so Gund took the device on their journey.

Another reason they did not long to return home.

A message did arrive after the titan fell from the sky. The message projected Chaxo's image onto any flat surface using what Gund had learned to be a hologram. The withered patriarch greeted Gund but then chastised them for taking the communicator away from the bond. Despite this, Chaxo was optimistic and declared music somehow affected the titan, and music would be how The Integration would subdue it.

The monster was called TAKER 7, and it contained creatures—humans. Chaxo also warned that alliances were not working well and that many things were complicated between the many forces within the people among the stars.

The Integration would be Chaxo's home for the foreseeable future, and he didn't know when or if he would return. The message ended with Chaxo telling Gund not to follow and to return to the Red Mountains once their journey into the rain-forest was complete. It filled Gund with a deep sadness, but they were glad to have the message to replay whenever loneli-ness crept in.

Gund longed to join their patriarch but decided to finish their quest first since they would be showing up uninvited. This may also have been enough to forego the initiation, not that Gund planned to stay. Returning to their spawning pool, sinking beneath the soup of life, and emerging wholly changed inside and out was far more terrifying than the hulking monster in the distance.

Gund repeated the message, staring at their patriarch's holo-gram; his wide-set, bulbous black eyes and long, curvy smile were always the first things they noticed. Chaxo's bright red and blue stripes filled Gund with familial pride, as their stripes and spots were quite similar.

It was the color of their bond. The Corans from the Red Mountains all shared some variant of this color pattern, but Chaxo and Gund were the only ones with stripes. The rest of Gund's bond had all developed dots or faded splotches.

Gund turned the communicator off and sighed. The thin air this high was delightful, and the night songs of the creatures below relaxed their mind. They placed the device back into their satchel and closed their eyes, dreaming of one day joining their patriarch on the great adventure above. How proud Chaxo might be of Gund for subduing such a foe.

A sudden gust of wind interrupted Gund's daydream. A massive starquill raced past them. Thirty or so of the gigantic birds followed a twisting single-file path behind the leader. Gund froze. The river of pink feathers snaked toward and around the titan, the flock paying it no mind, disappearing one by one behind the dormant TAKER 7.

The starquills flew higher than even dragons could reach and, therefore, had no natural predators and paid no mind to anything other than their destination—a remote island in the north. Nothing could touch them at this great height; most Corans considered them sacred.

It was a blessing to be so close, and Gund took their migration path as a confirmation.

The barrel-chested Coran shouldered their banruu and climbed down the twisting tower, passing several empty pods along the way. Once on the ground, Gund leaped toward the slumbering giant, dense rainforest giving way to flattened barren lands. Any flora and fauna existing here a season ago had either fled or was now a part of the pulverized waste Gund now tread upon.

A sporadic assortment of lakes lay before them as TAKER 7's footprints had made deep pools near the river, the water flowing between each depression. Gund stopped at the edge of one of these strange lakes to climb upon a jagged boulder of red stone jutting out of the ground. After taking a deep breath, Gund positioned the banruu underneath their fleshy jowls and set their six-fingered webbed hands to playing.

The large double-necked instrument was fashioned from the cavernous skull of a Fangslug, and its heavy strings were crafted from the dried gut fibers of the exact creature. The skull's two prominent tusks were filed down enough to act as a crook for Gund to rest their arm while playing. The downward flaring lateral nasal cavities of the Fangslug were the only openings in an otherwise watertight skull. They projected the music, Gund plucking at the bass strings first, attached to the thicker wooden neck. The thinner parallel neck above was shorter and would come in later after Gund laid the piece's foundation. The two fretless necks and mottled skull were well-worn but cared for.

The banruu was as much a friend to Gund as any of their bond and had been with them longer than anyone else. Gund plucked at the familiar strings with their calloused yet nimble fingers. There was no attempt to hide from the colossus.

This would end in glory or death.

Rich, bass-heavy tones thundered out across the artificial lake. Gund waited for the sound to reverberate back before playing again, striking the thick strings to accompany the returning echoes. Within moments, they fell into a trance, rocking on a remnant of the Red Mountains, playing a gentle call-and-response tune to the still juggernaut beyond. The invader's destruction had left a deafening silence in its wake, and Gund's banruu now filled it with song.

"We've never played in such silence before, have we?" Gund spoke aloud. Their voice would have sounded like a random mix of croaks, grumbles, and tongue chirps to a human. "I prefer to blend and dance with the sounds of the world around us. Jel, I hope your voice climbs deep inside this strange monster," Gund croaked. They played deeper riffs from the banruu. The lake danced with illumination. Aquatic glowworms started to surface, attracted by the booming sounds of the instrument. Gund smiled. "That's a good start."

Once enough thick layers of bass were set, Gund strummed at Jel's smaller set of strings. They walked their fingers down the fretboard, creating an improvised ambient melody nestled between the lulls of deep overtones. Gund rocked side to side with their eyes barely open, moving one or both hands to play a continuous loop.

A dense fog enveloped the bottom half of the titan, obscuring it somewhat. The mass of glowworms had increased in size, squiggling in unison after each heavy strum. The sky darkened. One of Cora's moons sank beneath the horizon, yet Gund continued to play their tune under the scant starlight.

The lights in the sky stopped dancing. Gund closed their eyes. The music droned on, and time disappeared, the Coran swaying with their song.

The outside world faded into the darkness, and Gund was entirely left unaware as TAKER 7 turned its head toward the player on the rock.

"LISTEN, mate. As you requested, " Morna is down there trying to hide TAKER 7 since Coran was somehow able to put the beast to sleep with a song it learned from Kels," Crumb mumbled over the comms connected to his helmet. That's all I have for you."

It was hard to believe the bugger was able to lull the titan to sleep with a simple song. It must have been quite a tune.

A hiss of static was the reply, and Crumb sighed at the bandwidth meter, indicating how slow the response would be. He glanced at the void sensor display, which remained silent. There were no starcraft in orbit outside of Cora. Crumb tapped on the image of the planet within the display, and the void sensor scanned the planet's surface, pinging when two void engines were discovered. One belonged to the damaged carrier of TAKER 5, and the other to Kels' ship, The Distant Memory, which was hovering nearby. Kels was lingering, and the longer she stayed, the more danger she put herself and her crew in.

"Understood," a warbling digital voice crackled into Crumb's earpiece. "My sources tell me that Paran is sending another TAKER to intervene. I don't know which one. I'd expect the carrier to arrive soon and a detachment to destroy anything in their way. I'd tread cautiously, and might I remind you that you aren't the only one after this bounty."

Crumb rolled his eyes and tapped on the void sensor to resume monitoring the orbital space around Cora. The planet's two shepherd moons staggered one another, cutting the shimmering ring around the superplanet into three distinct sections. The segmented rings were patterned in muted shades of ice, rock, and dust. Crumb admired the luminous display, smiling.

"When do I get paid?" He responded to the voice, still smiling. Crumb pressed against an indentation on his silver helmet and spoke to his ship. "Mouse, show me more of the rings," Mouse responded by activating tiny thrusters to tilt the cockpit forward, giving Crumb a much fuller view of the shimmering rings. "Ta," Crumb said, letting go of his helmet. The cockpit was tight but cozy, shunting out from the rest of his starcraft into a massive translucent orb surrounding it. Crumb pressed his knee against the ship controls, spinning the cockpit to keep his view unchanged. The ship drifted far outside Cora's orbit, cloaked and waiting.

"The amount will depend on you as soon as you reach The Altacruz. Temple, the AI inside TAKER 7, must be recovered and remain intact. If you can, recover both TAKER 5 and TAKER 7. The survival of their crew is not of the greatest concern, but you would be paid extra for each surviving crew member. I'll also include exploratory rights of the green exclusion zone if you do recover TAKER 7 and a bonus if you can recover TAKER 5. I have carriers on standby to recover them once you send word." Crumb smiled ear to ear, his cheeks starting to hurt. "Don't forget TAKER 7's Constellation is still hovering somewhere among the rings of Cora, and if they come online as I assume they will, you will have to deal with them too. If you cannot recover Temple somehow, I wouldn't come back." Crumb's smile wavered.

"Understood, Kali, no need to get drastic," Crumb said, checking the void sensor. "I'll look forward to seeing you and the bloody payment when I return. Ta." Crumb waited until the green flickering of a successfully sent message notification appeared on the edge of his visor before severing the secure comms channel. He flipped up a row of crimson switches in the cockpit to bring the sleeping thruster engines online, warming them up in hopes the ship's cloaking wouldn't falter. The cloaking held, but an abrupt burst of void portals opening nearby caused the pilot to jump in his seat, bumping the controls and sending the ship backward.

"That was fast..." Crumb whispered to himself, re-aligning his targeting system to the nose of the carrier rupturing through the open portal. It was fascinating to watch the event unfold, the massive ship reanimating itself, leaving the void behind. The pilot put his hands behind his helmet, waiting patiently for each ship to arrive.

Three ships spit from the open void, one massive carrier with a silver TAKER in its clutches and two hunter ships. The hunter ships were known as Blackstarts, bioweapons with an innate ability to track void engines. Their serpent-like bodies flanked the carrier. The Blackstarts were for the ships on Cora. The carrier was doomed, but they tended to be light on crew and had hopefully already abandoned ship.

Crumb slapped the steering controls toward the planet, prodding the void sensor. He selected The Distant Memory and replicated its void signature with a crude toggle installed near an empty cavity in the cockpit. Within moments, Mouse started emitting the same void signature as The Distant Memory.

"Time to tempt the snake." Crumb de-cloaked and fired up Mouse's thrusters to full speed, diving toward the trio of ships that had arrived. Mouse was fast, and soon Crumb was upon the three ships, taking full advantage of his translucent canopy to verify which TAKER had arrived. "Not what you signed up for, eh, Rez?"

Crumb positioned Mouse flush against TAKER 3's carrier ship, extending nimble crab-like appendages from Mouse's underbelly. The tiny pincers flailed until they found the curved, heavily armored cooling pipes jutting along the carrier's smooth surface. Crumb touched the indentation on his helmet again.

"Let's get our backup plan going. Bite this sodding scrap heap," he said while looking at the heat signatures of the two Blackstarts. One had already begun its dive for the planet's surface, but the other lingered behind, its movement confused. The bioweapon jerked toward the planet and then back toward Crumb's position. Crumb couldn't help but burst into laughter, watching the ship wiggle in confusion.

"Paran, you've outdone yourself with these monstrosities!" He cackled. Mouse had pierced the massive heat pipe with a small quantum beam welder. A moment later, Mouse produced a needle, crafted with the same material as TAKER 3's silver body, to fill the cavity. A hyper-coagulant was injected into the carrier's liquid coolant supply, and once complete, Mouse retracted the needle. The quantum beam welder sealed the cavity and disappeared inside the Mouse. The whole ordeal was over in less than a few minutes.

Crumb smirked, pulling at a green handle to retract the claws attaching him to the infected carrier. "May your gifts be his."

He took the reigns of his starcraft and pressed the thrust down hard with his foot, scorching the carrier's shiny surface as he blasted away from it. He tapped the targeting computer and locked onto the confused Blackstart, the twisting ship spiraling into view. Crumb could see its jagged maw with unnerving clarity, the head of the bioweapon sporting a single shimmering tusk. Beneath the protruding horn was the rest of the head, two sets of cloudy white eyes, and rows of ceramic razor teeth. Crumb drew close to the creature, feigning movements similar to those he'd witnessed The Distant Memory perform in his training simulator. Mouse chimed with a warning indication of target lock, which put a smile on Crumb's face.

"Gotcha."

Crumb slammed his foot on the thrust brake and pulled hard on the controls, twisting Mouse around so he could target the infected carrier. Sweat dripped from the pilot's forehead. He glanced toward the radar field, tracking the now encroaching Blackstart, which was picking up speed. It was faster than Mouse but nowhere near as agile. Crumb clenched his teeth, throttling toward the carrier, almost skittering across the ship's surface but managing to change direction before impact. The Blackstart targeting him also attempted to pull away, but it was too late. The serrated tusk stabbed into the carrier, activating the serpentine ship's self-destruct sequence. The single powerful thruster hidden within its belly protruded, firing at full burn, thrusting the spear deeper into TAKER 3's carrier. Crumb smiled. He slowed Mouse to hover over the erupting chaos, pumping his fist in the air. The Blackstart bit into the armored carrier, its core overheating. It was never not fun to outwit these simple creatures.

Crumb pulled away from the imminent void engine explosion when a snarling voice crackled into his ear.

"Kels! The Yanarthans have arrived and will protect you! Fall back, and let us handle this!" A gravelly voice bellowed through the comms.

"You've got to be-" Crumb's complaint was cut off by a sea of bright explosions erupting behind his field of view, causing him to wince.

"For Yanaria!" Another random voice came through his helmet, and Crumb dropped the void signature of The Distant Memory, reverting back to Mouse.

"I'm not Kels, you dumb cat, it's me, Crumb!" The pilot barked into the comms, turning to face the fading wall of white flare explosions. Within moments, no less than twenty fighters emerged from the white curtain, the pack leader in an upgraded version of the standard Yanarthan fighter.

It was Krynn. Of course, it was Krynn.

The fighters broke formation once they neared the carrier, pelting the now shredding ship with colorful pulse cannons, which did nothing to damage the carrier's armor. The frenzied Blackstart ignored the useless pulse fire, still busy with its task. Instead, the bursts of prismatic weapons splashed the ships with color, each fighter having their own individual pigment to help ensure bragging rights as to which was able to deal the final blow. It wasn't long before the entire carrier was a rainbow of colorful burn marks, swarmed by a tenacious detachment of delusional Yanarthans.

"Get away from that carrier! It will explode any minute once that Blackstart's void engine overheats!" Crumb barked into his comms.

"Krynn does not retreat, even in the face of death," a calm voice replied. "Perhaps we would not be here if you hadn't baited us with your false void signature, coward."

Crumb sighed and closed his eyes. Cheers of victorious bloodlust filled his helmet, bits of the carrier sloughing away from where the Blackstart was still chewing. "Looks like it's your lucky day, Rez."

Crumb grumbled, touching the side of his helmet, "Mouse, cut the horn from that snake."

Mouse burst into action, flying right into the plasma fire that tapered away once Crumb's ship approached.

"Get out of the way!" A random pilot snarled over the comms. "That is *my* target!"

Ignoring the request, Mouse used the same crab-like claws to clamp atop the Blackstart and went about severing the serpent's horn, still buried deep inside the carrier. Mouse's tiny quantum beam welder snipped the terrible spear from the Blackstart's head, and, despite its thrashing, Mouse fired its thrusters, carrying the doomed bioweapon away from TAKER 3 and its colorful carrier. When there was enough distance between them and the carrier, Crumb released the ship and thrusted away.

"Whenever you're quite finished with this ludicrous display," Crumb growled, "I'd suggest you bugger off before this snake takes you all with it."

Finding itself free from the Blackstart, the carrier ship corrected course and trudged toward Cora, its engines over-heating from the coagulant Mouse had injected earlier. It could reach the planet's surface, but it would not fly again once it landed without significant repair.

The frantic Blackstart spiraled in sporadic directions, and the entire squadron of Yanarthan fighters peppered it with colorful cannon fire. Despite their weapons being unable to do any damage to the thing, they were successful in pushing the ship, as the barrage of rainbow bolts sent the now glowing serpent further away from the Cora until its void engine reached the maximum threshold and burst, spilling forth a cloud of void resin erupting in streaks of lustrous purple liquid. The Yanarthans continued firing until the void resin exploded, causing a chain reaction that tore the entire bioweapon into star-dust, with purple energy waves billowing from the center of the explosion.

The Yanarthans cheered in unison. Crumb shook his head. He steered Mouse away from the pointless victory, the carrier hauling TAKER 3 still meandering toward Cora's surface on a trajectory for TAKER 5. He frowned. Perhaps they would need to wake TAKER 7; there was no way Morna could handle Rez one-on-one.

Crumb sat back, glancing at pin-ups of scantily clad alien and human women decorating the periphery of his cockpit. Once he found the lady he sought, he pulled the picture down and set it on the cockpit dashboard. "Sweet Aliz, can you help me figure out what to do?"

The crumpled picture said nothing in reply, but her sultry smile and skimpy clothes put the tiniest smirk on his face. Crumb studied the outfit Aliz was wearing, moving from her cleavage down to her hips, then further down her dark and shimmering legs before glancing up at her eyes. Crumb wiggled his eyebrows. She held an instrument, a silly prop matching her equally ridiculous yet alluring costume. Crumb stared longer at the instrument than anything else.

"Ha!" Crumb cackled, snatching the photo from his dashboard, pressing the paper against his helmet, and attempting to kiss the tiny musician. "I knew you could do it, Aliz!"

Crumb returned Aliz amongst her friends and tapped his hand against his helmet.

"Mouse, patch me into a comm link with The Distant Memory. I need to speak to Kels," he said, a smile growing on his lips. The adventure awaiting him in the green exclusion zone, a place no human had ever been, made his heart flutter. A static hiss and green light appearing in his visor's periphery confirmed his connection with The Distant Memory.

"Crumb? Is everything okay up there? We've just lost TAKER 5's carrier, but they've been able to hide TAKER 7 until we figure out how to get them out of here. I saw explosions in the sky and feared the worst," Kels said, calm in her voice despite everything still unfolding.

"TAKER 3 made it through and is on the way to the surface. The Blackstart meant for you has been taken care of," Crumb said, grinning, with a pause allowing for gratitude that never came. "We need to wake TAKER 7 if there is any hope for you or TAKER 5."

"How?" Kels said, a tenseness in her voice catching Crumb off guard.

"Tell me, do you still have that instrument with you? The one you used to teach Gund that song?" Crumb asked. "Otherwise, we might need to lean on the amphibian..."

"Yes, our kana flute is still aboard our ship," Kels replied. "Why?"

"So you can wake up the sleeping giant. We need their gifts."

TO BE CONTINUED...

The adventure continues in the upcoming novel TAKERS

ACKNOWLEDGMENTS

This book would not exist without the support and encouragement of many people:

To Becky, who endured many late-night writing sessions and endless discussions about characters—thank you for your patience and belief in me.

I am deeply grateful to my writing group, B2B Writing Group, whose feedback helped shape this story into something more substantial.

To the friends and family who offered insights and encouragement, your words meant more than you know.

Finally, to those who inspire me daily, whether through books, films, music, or the vast wonders of the universe, this is for you.

ABOUT THE AUTHOR

Logan Sroufe is an author residing in Cincinnati, Ohio. He composes his works with the enthusiastic support of his wife, children, and furry companions. He has published works with the B2B Writing Group and is committed to crafting narratives that transport readers to new realms.

Stay connected for updates at **www.logansroufe.com**

 tiktok.com/@sroufewriter

 instagram.com/sroufewriter

facebook.com/sroufewriter

www.ingramcontent.com/pod-product-compliance
Lightning Source LLC
Chambersburg PA
CBHW050458110726
47899CB00003B/994